Trio Trails

Adventures in Delhi

Vaneeta Vaid

KNOWLEDGE WORLD

KW Publishers Pvt Ltd
New Delhi

KNOWLEDGE WORLD

KW Publishers Pvt Ltd

4676/21, First Floor, Ansari Road, Daryaganj, New Delhi 110002

E knowledgeworld@vsnl.net **T** +91.11.23263498 / 43528107

www.kwpub.com

ISBN 978-93-80502-94-6

One

"Drat! Can you believe that? We are shifting again! *To Delhi!*"

Piffy and Miffy sat up at this news, when Biffy their sister pranced into the cottage, into their room, without breaking a step, one fine sunny morning. Miffy, Biffy and Piffy are identical triplets. They look so much alike that it is difficult to tell them apart. To introduce them, they are eleven years old and love solving detective adventures! They have recently moved from Mumbai to Shimla. Shimla has already given them a spine tingling adventure which launched them as pretty smart detectives!

Presently, catching her breath, Biffy gasped further, "Papa's Fish Mignon did it!"

"*What?*" the other two squealed together.

"Well, the MD of the hotels was visiting Shimla, and Papa, the great chef, created Fish Mignon and Vala," here Biffy pirouetted, smacked the tips of her fingers and continued, "The MD was sold and he posted Papa to Delhi so he could continue to eat fish the way Papa makes it!"

"BOWWW BOW BOW BOW!" What appeared to be a bullet was actually Rock, their tiny Chihuahua dog returning from his morning walk; he heard the commotion in the bedroom and shot through the door in full curiosity, *not wanting to be left out of any 'happening' outside or inside the house, you see!* His miniature, nine-inch-tall frame allowed him to fly or literally sail effortlessly onto the bed, plumb between the girls.

"Ha ha ha!" laughed the girls, nuzzling and petting Rock all at once!

"So you heard?" Malti, their in-house help said softly, entering, with a bundle of washed clothes weighing heavily in her arms.

"Malti Didi ....*Delhi?*" Piffy cried.

"Delhi ...yes....Madam just told me, she was planning to break the news at breakfast to you three. Biffy, of course, overheard, so you know now!" Malti smiled and put the clothes on the bed and began folding them neatly.

The girls, with the burning thought of shifting and leaving, went about getting ready for breakfast.

They had moved to Shimla from Mumbai last year, in the month of March and, of course, had very eventfully started their stay here (TRIO TRAILS BOOK -1). Schooling in Shimla was a different experience for these girls who were identical triplets. Shifting from Bombay to Shimla was quite a change. In fact, the ultra modern style of studies of Bombay did not apply here at all. There was a different approach to notes, classes and homework for the Shimla students. The girls adjusted, however, and were beginning to enjoy school. Their class teacher, Miss Neha Sharma, had made quite an impression on them. Pretty Miss Sharma was fascinated by the "Trips" (as they were fondly called) with identical looks. The Trips quickly became very popular, since, in spite of the staid and studious attitude of their class, these girls played pranks that lightened the mood considerably. From the first day onwards, the Trips confused everyone, whether it was one girl or three separate girls attending school! Finally, the school realised that they were triplets and that too, identical! Moreover, everyone had heard how these three had solved the mystery of Sethji's "housenapping" and hostage-like situation drama! Their bright, fun-loving outlook disarmed everyone and made them well known all over school!

Now, the girls were at home since the summer vacations were on.

Marching into the dining room of the picturesque cottage

and its surroundings, the girls chorused, "Mommy, when are we leaving?"

Mrs Lal smiled and heaved the kettle on to the stove. She was quite refreshed by her morning walk out in the woods and it showed in the spring in her step.

"Now, now, girls…let me be the one giving out details….Biffy you spoiled the surprise!"

"Mommy…tell, na!" Biffy picked up a toast and buttered it, simultaneously cajoling her mother.

"Let me correct you Biffy..*we are not permanently shifting to Delhi*…only for a month…now…. during your summer hols…. Papa has to attend a chef's conference and a chef skill enhancement capsule."

"Mommy, is it true that Papa's Fish Mignon" Piffy pronounced the word with difficulty, "has made us shift…Biffy said so!"

"Yes. "Mrs Lal giggled, "The MD ate the fish and recommended Papa for this very prestigious capsule." She was quiet for a while, then softly intoned, "But I can't help feeling a little irked, I wanted to spend the summer in Shimla..it has sort of grown on me…this place!"

"We will be back sooner than later…don't be disheartened!" Mr Lal boomed as he entered the dining room.

"Good morning, Papa!" the girls sang.

"Bow bow bowwwwww!" Rock added his greetings too.

"Sunny side up coming for the great chef," Mrs Lal trilled as she cracked an egg into the frying pan. The girls were downing orange juice, toast and cereal. "When do we go?" Mommy asked over the sizzle of the frying egg.

"Two weeks…ab Dilli door nahi!" (Delhi is not far now!) Papa Lal chuckled as groans and moans filled the air.

"What about school?" Biffy asked over the crunch of her toast.

"What about school?" Papa returned the question with a

question, "You will be back......we are just going for a.. um…" Mr Lal squinted and mentally calculated, "for over a month; school is not an issue…unless you girls don't do your holiday homework!"

"Papa!" Biffy admonished lightly.

Their vacations had just begun and moving to Delhi sounded fussy and tiresome. They had made new friends and were looking forward to spending the summer with them. Now this visit to Delhi had spoiled it all.

So the response to a holiday in Delhi was lukewarm.

"We were going to meet Dada-Dadi at Mumbai at the end of this month, remember?" Piffy put in, dusting off toast crumbs from her jeans.

The girls missed their grandparents and could not quite hide their disappointment.

"Yes… *but we are going to make it to Mumbai,*" Papa stressed, adding, "I have planned to snatch a week in Mumbai….before returning to Shimla….Even if you girls miss some school!" Papa assured them.

That cheered the girls a little.

Mr. Lal's parents lived in Mumbai. Though they all were in regular touch by phone, Mumbai seemed very far off as compared to Delhi. "Mommy, why do we have to shift too…can't Papa attend the conference alone?" Miffy asked.

"He can, but why should he? I want to be with Papa and I am sure so do you…am I right? It will be fun…Delhi has a lot of places to see! From there, we go to Mumbai! It can't be all that bad? So, now cheer up! Stop imagining the worst always!"

That silenced all protests and breakfast continued in peace.

Two

They were driving down to Delhi in their car. Rock was also accompanying them and going by air or train posed difficulties as no one wanted Rock to be in the cargo held, where pets have to travel in both these modes of transport; so the road route to their Delhi destination won all the votes hands down!

"Lucky, we are staying at the smaller hotel where we can keep the dog too," Papa had explained.

After some hours of driving through hilly curving roads, they reached the plains. By early evening, they had entered Delhi; the girls were asleep, since the journey's exhaustion had caught up with them. Rock nicely nestled in between, snored away too!

Malti squeezed into a corner with the Trips, gazed out of the car window, admiring the wide roads and network of flyovers of the capital city Delhi late in the evening. Finally, they reached the hotel, their home for the next month.

"This is such a small hotel!" exclaimed Miffy.

"Yes, the main hotel is miles away...in the city....this is a smaller place...we usually have conferences here....a smaller staff too." Papa said beckoning to the bellhop to take their luggage out from the boot of the car.

The hotel was plush, but very homely too. They entered a cosy lobby.

"Mr Lal-llll!" came a sing-song voice.

"Grwwwwol!" Rock snapped, staring ominously at the stranger who sailed forth from the offices behind the front desk.

"I am Mr Kalra! Manager complete, for this hotel! Or should I say for this inn? And I am the innkeeper?"

He flourished his hand pompously, then giggled, "Hyuk,hee hee, hyuk hyuk!"

Mr Kalra giggled in a nervous snivel-ly way. He giggled irritatingly even more when he saw the Trips. The whole situation seemed quite comical as he sucked his teeth and cried, "Ohh oh, three twins….look alikes…ho ho!"

"Triplets, actually," Biffy drawled, wondering why he was calling them twins.

Staring at his checked shirt, baggy loose trousers and minuscule cheeky moustache, followed by short hair, slicked to gel perfection, the girls had difficulty in keeping a straight face. His way of speaking too tickled their funny bones and made them want to guffaw out loud. They did not do that, of course.

"The rest of the members are staying in the main hotel…but you …aaaah growly pet," Mr Kalra pointedly looked at Rock who stared back murderously at him, "Sniff…yes, because of the pet, you have to stay… Um … here!"

He rolled his hands stylishly, clapped them and smiled ingratiatingly, "But it is my pleasure to welcome you…aaah…." He opened and closed his thin lips like a guppy.

Papa nodded and formally extended a hand, as did Mama. The moment where the Trips would have rudely chortled and burst into uncontrollable mirth passed thankfully and everyone got busy moving to the suites at the back of the hotel.

Mr Kalra began to tell them how five years ago, the hotel was given a makeover and fully renovated. "Before that, the rooms were very old fashioned, and not too modern….wiring…fittings… everything was changed……"

Mr. Lal nodded. This information had been provided in his brief before he came to Delhi.

Three

"What a shady character!" Biffy whispered fiercely to her sisters when they reached their rooms. "He is not a good fellow, believe me, this manager Kalra. There is something about him...I am sure he is hiding something," Biffy tapped her finger on one cheek and surmised thoughtfully.

"Biffs, now the mysteries are over! You are in Delhi so stop investigating!" Miffy teased her as she buttoned up her night suit.

Piffy threw a smile over her shoulders. Piffy sat by the dressing table, slowly brushing her hair, listening to the exchange. Malti had told her that brushing it at night assured good healthy hair.

Biffy picked up a tube of foot cream and squeezed out a portion on to her palm and began to rub her heels, thus, ignoring Miffy's teasing. Biffy loved solving mysteries. Her hunches had solved one mystery at least...in Shimla. Her gusto caught up with her siblings and they joined her eagerly too!

"What a small hotel....but our room is OK!" Biffy straightened and observed.

"Where are Mama and Papa?" Piffy asked Malti who entered with Rock.

"They are at the coffee shop. They are having dinner with the manager; they asked me to tell you to order from room service!"

Rock flopped in front of the air-conditioning vents. The vents, were high but he had smartly identified the coldest location in the room and settled himself there.

"Hello, room service...please send up three ham /chicken/

cheese club sandwiches, French fries, lots of ketchup and ice cream with cold coffee to room 311," Biffy succinctly instructed into the phone.

Malti gasped. Junk food was not allowed. But she was quiet since the girls were feeling disturbed by the change of place and a bit of high calorie food would definitely cheer them up.

Maintaining a silence, she helped the girls prepare for bed, after dinner, of course. Later, opening a packet of dry dog food, Malti filled Rock's bowl. He crunched, munched his food with healthy satisfaction.

Malti would be served food at the hotel staff canteen. Special permission had been granted to her for eating meals there.

"Burp!" went Biffy, signifying her complete approval for her hearty dinner, and reached out for her toothbrush. "Hey Biffs, after you have brushed your teeth, tell me, then I shall use the loo." Miffy called and took the opportunity to laze a bit more.

"Twoot….splash…phewtttoo ….okeeee!" Biffy voice sailed forth over her brushing.

Piffy grinned from under the covers, straddling a book crookedly, trying to read. She was all toothbrushed and clean by now. Rock too had settled himself.

After a while, the girls chatted sleepily.

"Wonder if they have computers…."

Biffy drowsily ventured,

No sound… as the other two, were fast asleep.

Four

"Computer!" Biffy awoke with that thought. Oh how she had missed good internet connectivity at Shimla. Because of the weather, the mountains, something or the other always disrupted services there. Scrambling out of bed, Biffy entered the adjoining room where Malti had her bed, though Malti was nowhere in sight. Picking up the internal phone, Biffy asked, "Can you tell me where I can find a computer in the hotel?"

Ten minutes later, Biffy walked down the corridor of the floor they were staying in and entered the Business Centre. Swiping her room key card, she entered the plush environs. A small introductory space comprised the reading area. In another room, six cubicles, facing a wall, housed six computers. The cubicle space was enough only for a computer desk and a swivel chair.

Seeing that three computers were occupied by other hotel guests, Biff sat down in front of an empty one. For the next half hour, she floated into cyber world happily!

Later, they all went down for the buffet breakfast to the coffee shop. The breakfast menu was a sumptuous one! Hot cinnamon rolls, orange juice, eggs and bacon, were the order of the day.

"Papa, why is that manager so ....eeeks?" Biffy asked inquisitively.

Biting into a roll, then almost choking on it, Papa glared at Biffy, then cautiously looked about. "*Biffy!?!*" Papa hissed, "He could well have heard us....where are your manners?"

"Oh sorry..." then she lowered her voice "Papa admit it, you think so too?"

Papa shrugged and said," Please don't put words in my mouth."

Piffy and Miffy arched an eyebrow at Biffy, but she refused to look at them.....her 'mystery' antennas were tingling!

"Biffs..where are the girls?" Mama came into the room looking for them. She still was in her "kaftan" nightdress. Stretching out her arms, not waiting for an answer, Mama said happily, "Ohhh luxury…no meal planning…just a walk to the coffee shop or the restaurant, and voila, tasty, exotic food!"

"But I prefer your cooking, mommy wommy!" Biffy got off the chair and spontaneously hugged her mother. Touched by this unexpected compliment, Mama hugged her right back. Tousling her hair, Mama said in a pleased way, "I wuv you too my gooli wooli woo!" Mama sighed in contentment and gurgled, "We are going to make the most of this holiday, are we not?"

Snuggling into her mother, Biffy muffled a "Sure Mommmy!"

Yes, the girls and their parents were beginning to quite enjoy the holiday which promised to be full of lazy days by the pool, sight-seeing in the hotel's air-conditioned buses, and lots of computer games and reading! Biffy, however, remained restless, in fact, she got quite an admonishment from Malti one day.

It so happened that they were strolling in the back gardens of the hotel one afternoon. Whilst walking, Biffy was glancing over the hedge, to the side beyond, when she gasped and ran.

Startled at her sudden flight, Malti called, "What? Biffy! Stay with us!"

"There is a suspicious looking fellah….got to check!" Biffy yelled over her shoulders.

Malti irritated, snapped, "Biffy here. Right now!"

Sigh! Biffy was not listening.

Miffy and Piffy chorused in a call too, "Biffy," with a resigned sigh. Rock shot after Biffy and created pandemonium, jumping high and trying to loop over the hedge.

Biffy ignored them all and stretching up on her toes, she boomed, "Who is it?" Rock by now was choking with hysterical barks, trying to bounce over the hedge!

The quavering voice of an old man answered, "Me…Anwar, the kabadiwala" (junk buyer/seller).

Sheepishly, Biffy settled back on her feet, "Rock, stop it!" But Rock was growling, snapping and jumping. Biffy coughed, "Er… but why are you hiding behind the hedge?"

Meanwhile, Malti and the others caught up. Miffy lifted Rock up and shushed him. He continued to growl in a low tone, not at all appeased so it seemed!

Apologetically, looking at Anwar, Malti pulled at Biffy, hissing, "Leave the kabadiwallah alone Biffy!".

"Aw Malti Didi… er… nothing…… he looked…. I mean… odd… I can smell something wrong…silly though, I guess..I may be wrong!" Biffy thoroughly embarrassed, shrugged and was at a loss for an explanation!

Anwar, white-haired and weather-beaten, stood and mumbled, "I did nothing….!"

Malti nodded silently and without looking back, led her wards away.

"Biffy? Such poor behaviour?" Malti admonished.

Biffy walked beside her, head bowed.

"Biffs stay! No mysteries here.. just an old kabadiwallah!" Miffy giggled.

"Silly me….just thought he was crouching suspiciously…."

"Let it go, Biffs!" Piffy quietly said. "Let's enjoy our holiday… no mystery is going to fall into our…rather your lap…. Believe me……this is no adventurous holiday…just fun time holiday!"

"Yeah Biffs, cool it!" Miffy added.

Biffy shrugged, with apology writ all over her face, she hugged Malti.

Well Piffy, sorry you are wrong…events that are going to follow shall ensure that a very puzzling mystery will fall into Biffy's lap!

Five

"Hello! How was work?" Mrs Lal smiled when her husband walked in one evening into the children's room. "Work is good.... but this *hotel*? Something so strange is happening!" Mr Lal sighed, flopping on to an arm chair.

"What happened?"

"What is really troubling here is that some money is missing from the hotel accounts! Our guests' credit cards are being used without their knowledge"

"You don't say? How is that? Has someone stolen the cards or what?"

"No no...cyber crime...hacked or misled the guest into giving credit card details and swiped away money!"

"So are you not.....I mean, is the hotel not doing something about it?"

"Yes, the management is abuzz with this!"

"But why don't you report it?"

"And scare the customers away...no, we are discreetly trying to find out!"

The girls hooted at this, but Mr Lal could not be drawn into giving further details after that!

Biffy determinedly decided to snoop out the cause of all this. It was not long before she began sleuthing around.

Biffy began to spend much time at the Business Centre. The computer she sat at already had an account open, since someone had forgotten to log off. An e-mail letter actually was open. Biffy read it under her breath,

"Dear Sir,

We are mailing the catalogues at the earliest. Your request for a Rolex watch costing $.....has been processed and your credit card numbers...."

Biffy squinted, Rolex? Wow! "Savvyior. m@... she read the name of the account holder. "Very odd ID...who could it be?" Biffy muttered.

"Omigosh what high living..... this person must have money! Even I know a Rolex watch is mighty expensive!"

Biffy chuckled, signing off the account and signing into her own account.

Later, after breakfast, the Trips ventured into the lobby. Papa had left for his conference at the main hotel. Mama was lying down in since she was tired. Malti too was busy.

The Trips and Rock strolled around the lobby area. Today, the three girls were dressed alike.

Collared tee shirts, shorts, open sandals and hair tied up in a high pony tail. The colours of their clothes were different, of course.

Leaning at the front desk, Biffy chatted with the pretty receptionist called Shweta. Shweta initially barely looked up from the laptop she was tapping, when the Trips assigned their places by the front desk counter. Of course, she could not ignore the presence of the identical looking company for long! To make up for her inattention, after her initial surprise at seeing triplets, she chattered affectedly!

"Sorry, but I do remain under pressure...yes, we don't have *many guests* as of now...by mid-month, the occupancy will be full. This summer season is starting late-ish....Our guests are all from abroad."

The receptionist smiled hesitatingly when Biffy bluntly uttered, "Your manager...Kalra..... is so funneee..in an odd way."

"Piffy!" Miffy sweated in embarrassment, but Biffy did not notice. And as luck would have it, they were interrupted when Mr. Kalra, walking like a peacock, trooped into the lobby.

He gave the Trips and Rock a cold look, brushing aside any greetings. "Grwolllll" went Rock, his body tensing. Biffy patted him to be quiet. That made no difference to Kalra. Ignoring them, he walked around the front desk and with a curt "Come here!" to the receptionist, he disappeared into the offices behind the desk. Like a frightened rabbit, the receptionist ran after him.

"What a rude…" Miffy gasped

"I know…in front of Papa, he smiles so hard I thought he would swallow himself!" Biffy gritted.

"Oh dear…that was rude, was it not?" Piffy timidly added.

"I am telling you, this man is up to no good…no wonder that Shweta was so nervous….there is something highly suspicious about him I say…"

"Ooooff Biffy…he is arrogant….rude, but that does not mean he is a crook.."

"Quiet! I am the detective…and if I say so…"

"Oh ho really?…sez who…!" Miffy cried!

"Oh Biffy n-not fair…" Piffy reproached.

The Trips teased, pow-wowed verbally, walking into the gardens outside! Rock obediently trotted beside them. Once in the gardens, they settled themselves by a hedge. Piffy and Miffy began to admire the rockery on the side. Biffy flopped on a bench and her sisters joined her too. Biffy's attention was diverted from the surroundings in front of her, when voices floated up to her from behind the hedge.

"Are you sure?" A "twangy" voice cried over the garden noises..

The Trips, settling on a bench, realised that a man and a woman were talking beyond the hedge.

Though the Trips could not see the owners of the voices, they could hear the exchange clearly.

"$.....has been spent but I never swiped my card for that amount."

In the background, a car geared and noisily left.

"Did you ask the bank?"

"Yes, they confirmed the purchase of a Rolex....but it fails me...I never bought one. Anyways, I will confirm....it's late night in America...I'll wait for the morning!"

"Oh Mr Neil Rodericks...Ma'am!"

The shrilly voice of Kalra broke in.

"Oh Mr. Kalra.....how do you do..."

Their voices faded as they entered the hotel.

Miffy and Piffy were not concentrating on the voices, as Rock had dragged a long twig and presented it at their feet. Biffy at that point paid no attention to Rock, as her sisters were doing, she was totally absorbed with the conversation the voices had presented! Biffy popped her head above the hedge and she saw that they were sitting actually right next to the main doors of the hotel.

So that is why they, the Trips, unseen, could clearly hear all the conversation of a few minutes ago..... it was happening at the porch of the hotel!

Biffy was foxed. Something was troubling her. Piffy and Miffy began to play catch with the white shiny pebbles strewn on a pathway near the rockery. Rock pranced up and down excitedly! But Biffy sat deep in thought. Suddenly, she gasped.

"The Rolex.....the same cost.....?!? The e-mail? Did that have something to do with this? What a coincidence.....Papa spoke of the same problem...?!?"

Biffy excused herself, and went up to the Business Centre. She sat down at the computer. However, this time, no other e-mail opened except for her own. Gnawing her lower lip, Biffy impatiently switched off the computer then switched it on again. Again, no mail popped up.

"I am so curious....it is too much of a coincidence that he, *that,* foreigner is talking about a Rolex....same cost...um- um- um!" Biff began to think deeply.

"It is so strange...no one reported these thefts before... not only has money been stolen, but items are also missing from the hotel!" Mr Lal informed his wife over a cosy family dinner in their room one evening.

"Really?"

"Yes! Daylight robbery so it seems! One painting was missing from the main suite, but was found unframed, rolled into a muddy pit as if in an attempt to hide it at the edge of the gardens! That is not all..... then a copper planter from the lobby, and a month ago, money was stolen from the cash registers at the coffee shop... then the credit cards mystery! Somehow all this is unacceptable!" Mr Lal pierced his broccoli with his fork and shook his head.

"Papa, the money stolen from the hotel accounts...and these stolen items are all connected?"

"Nah...not to my mind!"

"Papa, why is the management not calling the police?"

"Hotels don't announce...ah.... *mismanagement*...our reputation is at stake! The management has strictly decided to cool off and not involve too much of police interference!" Papa informed them firmly.

"But Papa, that is so.... so..!" Miffy mumbled shocked.

Even Piffy thought it silly not to report the crimes in order to protect the hotel's reputation.

A healthy argument ensued.

Later in the afternoon, the Trips relaxed in the room. However, Biffy relaxed for a few minutes, then shot up from the bed and restlessly paced at first, then left the room hurriedly.

Miffy and Piffy looked up, a little surprised when Biffy walked out of the room, completely ignoring them.

The two were reading comics and digging deep into a large packet of potato chips.

Malti looked the other way at more digestion of junk food for her wards. "They are on holiday," she consoled herself more than once on this trip.

Miffy and Piffy did not fail to notice the purposeful look on Biffy's face as she raced out of the door.

Unaware of them or their piqued reactions, Biffy bolted through the carpeted corridor and not waiting for the lifts, ran down the service stairway.

I need to know who this thief is...I don't know what but somehow I feel I need to stand in the lobby and may be find something ... what... I don't have anything defined! Biffy's mind raced with these thoughts as she made her way to the lobby area.

Once she reached the lobby floor, she tried to look as nonchalant as her excited heart would allow her!

Soft, melodious music, and fragrant room freshener filled her senses as she arrived at the lobby. Now to work, thought Biffy, stepping up forward faster. But as soon as she entered, Biffy stopped short.

Sigh! The lobby was full. Two bellhops, three service personnel, some guests going to the two restaurants of the hotel, the receptionist at the desk, along with two other front desk managers. "Vroooom" the vacuum cleaners swept the already shiny floors. "Chatter- chatter", different levels of voices, intermingling with soothing western classical music, floating from overhead PA systems, filled the air. Everything fell into semi-silence when Biffy walked into the small lobby, *so it seemed to Biffy!*

"Hello little girl, now, which one are you?" greeted one.

"How chweet" went another. *"Is she one of those triplets?"* came another sally!

So on and so forth; in other words, Biffy was *noticed* and any thoughts of sleuthing around were effectively dashed!

Biffy grinned in a forced way and turned to run back to her room.

There is no way I can sneak around and not get noticed, Biffy thought.

"Aha, the sleuth is back!" Words attacked as soon as she entered. Arms akimbo, Miffy was glaring. Piffy, though with softer approach, managed to look peeved too.

"Whaaa?" Biffy was startled.

A silence full of touchy animosity, asking Biffy to explain herself, stood between her and her sisters!

Miffy raised an eyebrow, with an unsaid, "Well?"

"Um…you guys did not believe me so…"

"So you ignored us huh?" Miffy looked so mad that she could hardly get the words out "Look, Biffy…you wandered off alone but let it be said: we are detectives together…so….share with us everything always…I know you are up to some sleuthing…how could you not tell us huh? !" Miffy said in a stern, firm way.

Piffy gently added, "I know."

Biffy's facial expressions turned mulish and she grumbled, "You were not going to believe me anyways!"

"Sez who? Come on Biffy! Were you really thinking you could manage sleuthing on your own? We are the Trips…three, not one, d'ya hear?"

Somehow that calmed Biffy and she became contrite. In an apologetic voice, she muttered, "What was I thinking? The Trips are three, *not one*…sorreee… OK, let me tell you now." That was the thing about Biffy, if you explained things properly to her, she calmed down and her temper tantrum was over!

In the moments that followed, Biffy, albeit, sheepishly, explained her entire suspicions, leaving out nothing.

"Miffs, I have nothing…nothing, only a hunch and suspicions! But you have to agree, is it not a coincidence to read a mail and then hear the same thing….my bones feel something is wrong! Someone swiped cards for online shopping! I am suspicious! See, hotel property being stolen…money being stolen….boy, my detective antennas are tingling! Are you with me? Will you two also help me solve this mystery?" Biffy asked her sisters anxiously.

"Hmm….Biffs, what mystery? Though, yes it is quite tricky! And too much of a coincidence…" Miffy mused.

'I don't think so! Leave it be! Why are we fishing for trouble?" protested Piffy in an unnerved way.

"Oh Piffy, you mouse…if something in the world is wrong, we have to right it, na?" Miffy, a tad impatiently, silenced her sister.

Piffy, about to open her mouth, closed it abruptly.

"I have nothing to go by except a random e-mail and an overheard conversation, plus Papa's information! However, my detective hunches are tingling," Biffy repeated, trying to desperately make a point but not giving up the hope that Miffy would understand and agree that her suspicions needed to be investigated.

"So what do you suspect is happening?" Miffy murmured, thinking aloud.

Biffy chewed her lower lip and shrugged, "I dunno, but surely some hanky-panky and an inside job!"

"It could be that the foreigner has some hanky-panky going on abroad only… may be we are just stirring up trouble for nothing?" Miffy added uncertainly, then shook her head and as if coming to a decision said, "Anyways, I am in!"

Piffy piped in,

"I- I don't understand….I mean we are not the police, so why do we court…d-danger?"

"Because, Piffy, we are serious detectives….now, we leave the choice with you…if you want out, say so..no hard feelings?" Biffy announced, matter of factly.

"Er," Piffy thought hard as the other two waited.

Then she shrugged and sighed, "I am in…my mind will always be wondering what you two are up to, so I may as be in!" Piffy said with an uncertain look.

Her sisters laughed and hugged her.

Six

"Look casual!" Biffy drawled under her breath to her sisters. It was early evening and they had strolled into the lobby area to sleuth! They had returned to the lobby with a plan you see!

Piffy controlled her nervousness by clenching her fists tight and walking stiffly.

"Unclench your fists!" Miffy hissed. That turned Piffy crimson red and she was visibly flustered.

Biffy drawled, "Leave her alone."

They had reached the reception when an interruption grabbed their attention. The interruption being Mr Kalra, the manager.

"Hello girls, welcome to the lobby again...but is it not bedtime for young girls??"

Kalra, in some hasty measures to make up for his past behaviour, spoke in a trilling, genial tone to the Trips as he emerged from his office. Biffy glared at Kalra, but Miffy made up for her sister's dour expression by smiling widely and saying, "Summer break, uncle... we have no bedtime deadlines! Our hols are on!"

"Hmm...OK, keep out of trouble, though." Saying that, Kalra sailed out of the hotel entrance door.

"I am following him!!" Biffy whispered.

"No, you cannot...!" Miffy grabbed her shoulder to halt her stride.

"Let go!" Biffy flung Miffy's hand off and dashed out too. Kalra had no idea Biffy was following him. He crossed the road and walked up to two streets away from the hotel.

Finally, Kalra stood under a lamp-post. He glanced suspiciously, here and there. Keeping out of sight, Biffy hid behind an autorickshaw. The wait was hardly ten minutes, when a car stopped. Looking here and there, Kalra jumped into the car, and was off! Biffy, heart beating wildly, watched the tail lights of the car disappear ahead. Confused at what she had just seen, Biffy returned to the hotel. Her sisters were livid at her behaviour, but they calmed down when she related what had happened.

"Gosh, why would he do that? I mean he could have called the car to the hotel...right?" Miffy asked.

"Some personal work...forget it..." Piffy said in a scared voice.

"He was really behaving suspiciously! I am going to check his office," Biffy broke in, ignoring Piffy.

"(Gasp) Biffy, no! You cannot check out his office...that is wrong!"

Piffy fiercely vetoed the idea; but no one noticed.

"What can we find there?' Miffy asked walking alongside her sister. Piffy hurriedly followed.

"I dunno...but let's just check. We may stumble on some clues......you never know!"

Biffy charted out a plan, "You engage the front desk receptionist at the extreme counter. I will slip in unnoticed inside."

So with this planning, the Trips approached the front desk receptionist.

"Hello", the Trips greeted the handsome young man manning the front desk.

"So you are on night duty?" Miffy charmingly smiled and inquired.

He returned the smile and began to chat. Miffy somehow led him to the extreme end of the counter. Piffy, looking nervous, followed suit. No one noticed Biffy slip into the offices behind the front desk counters!.

Hmmm, all wood and old fashioned, Biffy noticed as she crept into the office. But there were no carpets, and fancy Italian tiling covered the floor!

As she stepped in, she noticed a huge oak desk. On the desk was a laptop computer. Hurriedly, Biffy ran towards the desk. Going around the desk, just as she was going to check the laptop, a sound alerted her.

Oh no! Someone was coming!

With a dive, Biffy hid under the desk. Holding her breath Biffy crouched under the desk, praying that whoever it was would go away!

A whiff of lavender perfume assailed the crouching Biffy's nose. But she sat very still. She did not want to be discovered, you see. There was the tapping sound of high heels drubbed over the modern tiled flooring. They stopped at the desk. Biffy could not see anything but she felt the close presence of someone on the other side of the desk! Tense, Biffy sat motionlessly. The laptop was turned around and the only sound was the clicking of the keys. Then a ping, which Biffy could swear was a mobile message being sent.

The high heels "tick-tick-ticked" over to a file closet behind a screen that camouflaged the file cupboard.

What is happening? Biffy wanted to know. Unable to hold her patience anymore, Biffy slowly peeped up. She could not make out who was in the room. Especially since the screen hid her vision! But small sounds showed someone was going through the files *behind the screen*.

"I must leave…. whoever is here in the office is hidden behind that screen! This is my chance to leave…it is not safe to hang around anymore!' Biffy decided.

Sneaking in a bend, Biffy ran out, hoping no one had seen her.

Luckily, she left the offices safely!

"There she is!" Miffy exclaimed in a low drawl to Piffy when she sighted Biffy dashing out.

Oh yes, her sisters sighed in relief on seeing her slip unnoticed from behind the counter! They had been consumed with worry till then. Biffy nonchalantly sat on a lounge chair placed opposite the front desk counter. No one had noticed her either going in or coming out of the offices. Miffy and Piffy strolled up to her and sat down too. "I got nothing...however, someone came in and disturbed me."

"Who came in?!?"

"I really cannot say. I assume it was a female! Just could hear her fancy "tickety" heels! I could not see who it was! But I could sure smell her. Wow! Lavender perfume in a heavy dose! She is still inside...I slipped out!'"

"No probs, we can sit and wait...she has to come out from here only." Miffy assured Biffy.

But no one came out from the offices!

They waited and waited. Biffy thought even that was definitely very suspicious indeed! So when her sisters wanted to leave, Biffy adamantly refused.

"There is no other door to exit! Where did the lady disappear?" She argued "I want to wait and see...."

Miffy and Piffy dragged Biffy away. They were tired and sleepy. Sleuthing needed to be put on hold as of now.

Finally, though very reluctantly, Biffy left too.

Seven

"Hey, Hey…Rock!" Miffy pushed the overly energetic dog aside a few days later.

"Yawnnnnnn!" Whatsh time ish it?" Biffy groaned sleepily from under the covers.

"One o' clock in the afternoon," said a calm voice from the corner of the room.

"One o clock!" Piffy, Miffy and Biffy bounced up in chorus together.

"Yes. I have been sitting and sewing right here! I am happy for your triple action peaceful breathing—it acted like a symphony of music!" chuckled Malti, as she bit off the thread she was sewing with.

The Trips' pile of shirts and skirts that needed buttons fixed and hems stitched lay by her side.

"Oh Didi!"

"Well, if you watch late night movies…um detective movies…. you wake up late next day…all groggy and yawning.. not fresh at all!" Malti smiled, adding "But I am allowing it here..not in Shimla!"

The Trips sat up, rubbing their eyes and yawning!

Malti picked up the room service phone and ordered three glasses of milk.

Biffy did not get out of bed. She stared blankly at the ceiling.

These few last days she had closely been following Mr Kalra's movements around the hotel and nothing had come up. Biffy felt so frustrated. Everyone treated her like a cute little girl and laughed when she asked about the robberies, etc!

Piffy and Miffy chattered and tittered in drowsy wakefulness—tousling and rolling the overjoyed Rock who was the gladdest seeing them finally awake!

"Didi, where is Mama?" Miffy asked curiously, softly pummelling Rock off as he playfully tried to chew her hand.

Rock, yelping madly, ran off the bed and jumped up on the large table housing a lamp and the phone, via a chair, and woofed triumphantly!

"Ha ha ha ha!" They all laughed. Malti answered Miffy's query,

"Oh Madam is not here. Neither is Mr Lal. He is at the conference at the big hotel and she is with him. Some ladies coffee get-together today for her, you know, at the main hotel; kind of welcome organised by them to introduce her to some of the hotel wives." Malti paused then said, "Madam peeped in twice earlier—but had to leave—thus, allowing your extended slumber!"

Malti stirred in chocolate powder into the glasses of milk that had arrived and handed them one each. "Biffy get up....here drink your milk. What are you thinking about?"

Biffy self- consciously sat up and accepted her glass.

"Tbrrrriiiiiiinngggggggggg"

A shrill bell, followed by Rock's sharp barks, indicated there was someone at the door.

Malti stepped forward to open the door and let in a hotel staff member who loudly intoned, "There is some chaos going on in the lobby." He lowered his voice at Malti's raised eyebrow, "Madam rang up on the floor phone and sent a message that the children should be remain in the rooms till she returns. She could not get through...." His voice trailed as he glanced over Malti's shoulder to view Rock pawing the 'off the hook' handset on the table surface, squeakily barking!

Malti turned and clicked her tongue apologetically, "ROCK!" Excitedly, Rock left the phone and jumped on the chair to hysterically bark towards the man at the door! This detonated a series of giggles from Miffy and Piffy!

Malti stepped out of the room to speak to the person. Miffy hurriedly placed the phone back on the hook and lifted Rock off the chair as one would a baby.

Only Biffy seemed to be alert to what the hotel staff member had said.

"Chaos?" Biffy asked Malti sharply when she reentered the room.

"Hmmm..."

"Didi, what has happened?"

"I really don't know but you girls...whaaa...!?"

Biffy, without an "excuse me" side-stepped Malti and rushed out, *in her night dress!* Biffy apparently was rushing towards the lobby.

"NO!" Malti blocked Piffy and Miffy as they jumped up to follow Biffy.

Worriedly, Malti stepped out and peered down the corridor to spot Biffy. Biffy had vanished!

Meanwhile, Malti glared at the other two and growled, "I am going after her...*no one leaves the room, understood!*"

The two were shocked to hear the usually soft spoken Malti use such a stern tone. They meekly nodded and sat down on their beds. The effect of Malti's "NO!" was fastest on Rock who had receded to a corner and in a woebegone way, looked up with a sorry expression!

Eight

"This is crazy traffic!" Mrs Lal peered forward from the windscreen as they drove back to the hotel. "It has been forty-five minutes and we are still stuck here!" agreed Mr. Lal, irritation tingeing his voice.

"All this construction for the metro and flyovers… what about us, the commuters!"

"Hmmm!" Mr Lal nodded, negotiating the nose of the car slowly forward.

"Imagine…the chaos at the hotel!" Mrs Lal exclaimed, "Thankfully, I am returning with you….makes sense, out of respect, they cancelled the ladies meet…..I wonder what happened…?" murmured Mrs Lal, her eyes on the road ahead.

"Hmmmm! No details yet, once I get back, the full account can be ascertained," Mr Lal replied slowly.

Biffy, with single-minded intent, ran down the corridor and the service steps. On entering the lobby, she hesitated. "What happened?" Biffy whispered to one of the hotel bellhops standing by.

Her face turned white as the boy spoke.

Back in the car with Mr and Mrs Lal, the atmosphere was turning a little stressed. You see, Mrs Lal's mind rang with this warning signal: *if* Biffy gets a whiff…she would be on her mystery trail.. oh dear ………." Worriedly, Mrs Lal dialled her phone. Her nervousness increased when she could not be put through to the room extension….

At the hotel, Biffy stood ashen by the communicating doors towards the lobby. The staffer was jabbering still, like a gossip columnist giving out sensational news! Her mind picked up one morsel of information that the staffer had given: *Mr Kalra had been kidnapped!*

"Mr Kalra is missing…his family is crying foul….no one has seen him since last night after he left hotel…. may be he has been mugged and…may be… pssst" The staffer indicated a cutting movement near his throat, "slit in the throat…dead!" The staffer seemed to enjoy giving this graphic detail to Biffy who stood numb.

The police… are asking questions….ha ha, the hotel is trying to hush it down…bad publicity….!" The staffer babbled on. That is why no one noticed Malti come up behind Biffy.

"Come, come upstairs Biffy…right now." Malti soft, yet firm voice broke through Biffy's befuddled mind as she stepped up behind her. After making sure the other two girls were not pursuing her, Malti had followed Biffy to the lobby. With a confused nod, Biffy turned and followed Malti back to the room.

"Mr Kalra has been kidnapped, Miffy and Piffy!" Biffy croaked as soon as she returned to the room.

"You don't say!" Miffy gasped with a sharp intake of breath. Piffy sat on the bed staring at Biffy with a mix of fear and wonder.

"We have to know.. I mean…solve this thing…!"Biffy chewed her lower lip.

Piffy's face crumpled, "No Biffy, you are out of it….it is a kidnapping…stay away….bad…we are just children."

Biffy immediately sprang up and hugged her sister, "Piffy, it is all right. I am er-er.. we are, I mean ..*detectives*.. this is our job."

"Um..yes!" Miffy agreed though her voice was not very convincing.

"Job? Who employed you? Huh huh!" Piffy said with a slight break to her voice.

"Self-employed!" That broke the seriousness of the situation and they broke into giggles!

"Malti ....Bifffy.....Biffy..er Piffy- Miffy....!" Mrs Lal rushed in. Seeing all three girls together, she let go of a deep breath. Holding them, she mumbled, "I was so worried."

"Ma..but why?" Biffy asked wide-eyed.

Mrs Lal smiled indulgently and looked at her children with a complete mama expression of love. "Nothing... just like that!" she softly said.

"We know Kalra is missing." Biffy said clearly.

"Oh." Mrs Lal tried not to look flustered.

Biffy tried to question her mother but could not get any details. "Drat, how could my hunch about Mr Kalra...rather poor-poor Mr. Kalra be so wrong!" Biffy mused time and again. She was sheepish when her sisters kept up the "we told you so" expressions!"

Biffy felt her hunches had let her down. Instead of realising that Mr Kalra was on the good side, she had suspected him! Now he had been kidnapped. She was ashamed that she had been so critical of him to all and sundry!

I will find him. I owe him this! I need to gather clues myself, Biffy decided, with her lower lip jutting forward determinedly!

Nine

No one noticed the cute girl aimlessly playing around in the lobby. Joyfully swinging a yo-yo, Biffy did not give away her alert attentiveness. But nothing much came of the vigil. The police were not really giving much information. The mystery deepened. It had been four days now and Mr Kalra was nowhere to be found. No ransom note had been found either! The police was investigating but had apparently reached a dead end since no ransom note had come in! The hotel security had been beefed up outside. Generally, there was an air of 'something is going to happen' around the lobby area! Biffy was just deciding to leave when came a booming, protesting voice!

"I want to talk to some authority…..!" an Australian accented voice demanded at the reception. Biffy immediately sidled up to hear better.

"Ma'am…er we cannot know how your credit card shows more swipes…ask your… er banks!" Shweta the receptionist nervously tapped her computer keys on the laptop and simultaneously answered. This conversation was taking place at the front desk.

The Australian lady muttered an oath and stormed off.

"What is her problem?" Biffy boldly asked the obviously uncomfortable receptionist.

"Don't know." Shweta was staring at her laptop on the counter and tapping a reply message on her cyber chat box obviously; when the "sent" ping ensued, Shweta turned her attention to Biffy, "Funny, how these people, cannot account for how much credit they have used on their cards….why are they blaming the hotel?"

Biffy gave Shweta a long look. Shweta got quite uncomfortable. She turned self-consciously and began fussing with her other desk computer.

Without a word, Biffy left the front desk. The wheels of her mind were obviously working out something.

She was strolling in the gardens when she heard Mr Sud, one of the substitute managers for poor Mr Kalra, say to someone, "Things are serious.. but we need no publicity…"

Biffy's ears got alerted and she moved closer, trying to hear what was being said but they seemed to enter the hotel and disappear into its environs. Biffy shrugged, her mind thinking furiously.

The Trips gingerly made their way towards Mr Kalra's picturesque cottage the next day.

"Hello aunty…I er came to say how bad we are feeling that Mr Kalra is missing", Biffy official spokesperson, spoke for all. In their chase for clues on the kidnapping, the three detectives, prodded by Biffy, decided to call on Mrs Kalra. Procuring a free bunch of flowers from the discarded pile at the hotel lobby, the three minced their way down the lane towards the living quarters where Mr Kalra stayed. His house was a pretty cottage nestled amongst trees and blooming flower paths. Poor Mrs Kalra was quite bereft. She was also quite touched by the girl's concern.

"So sweet…Chef Lal's triplet daughters! Mr Kalra did tell me how alike you were…..oh dear…it has been four days, no news.. this is frightening…he had no enemies."

The Trips sympathetically listened to her trembling voice.

Mrs Kalra turned out to be very different from what they had imagined! Slim and tall, she was very smart and trendy. Wearing tight jeans and a loose blouse, she looked young and pretty. Her hair was tied in a pony tail, her feet shod in high heels.

The girls found her very fashionable indeed

"Er….did he seem upset or anything lately?" Biffy asked.

"On the contrary, he seemed happy," Mrs Kalra said, waving beautifully beringed-manicured hands. "You know, he was actually thrilled the other night ...the last night before he disappeared the next morning..." She paused sadly before continuing, "about some work which went off well... 'Brilliant plans will unfold and everything will happen right for...,' he said suddenly when we were eating dinner. My husband is a thinker and he suddenly speaks his thoughts aloud...I am quite used to it!" She smiled, then continued, "Anyhow I could not really understand since my husband hated to share his work talk with me. However, though he refused to explain...he seemed so happy." Misty-eyed, she sighed to say: "The next day, he (sigh) disappeared!"

"From office?"

"No, when I woke up, he was missing. No one has a clue where he went or from where he disappeared! I called the office and, oh dear, he was not there, and oh oh!" She silently sobbed into her kerchief.

Biffy and her sisters immediately patted and consoled her.

"So Mr Kalra most likely was trailing the robberies and thefts... his disappearance most likely is connected...!" Biffy mulled as they walked back to the hotel.

"Yes!" Miffy agreed.

"I was actually suspecting him of some connection with this whole thing...I wonder where he is? Isn't Mrs Kalra so 'haute couture', no?" commented Piffy. A discussion ensued on Mrs Kalra's high fashion looks and their voices faded as they walked towards the hotel.

Ten

"We are sleuths and we need info about all the goings on!" Biffy informed the smiling staff in the kitchens.

"Well, young girl or girls!" one trainee pointed to Piffy and Miffy, "two...um.... iron pots are missing and they walked out... ha ha ha!" he yelped, giggling helplessly. Frustrated, Biffy gave up and walked away! No one took her seriously!

It was past her bedtime when Biffy quietly got out of her bed. She slipped out of the room unnoticed and walked to the Business Centre on the same floor. The Business Centre housed a mini library and computers for the use of the guests.

Logging into her account, Biffy thought hard on what she wanted to do.

"Bing", a pop up message on her msn account popped up.

Biffy's heart beat faster. The pop up said it was a message from "Savvyior".

"Little girl, up so late?"

"Who is that?"

Biffy's hands flew over the keys.

"Now, would you not want to know?"

"Yes, please."

"Nah.....just popped to warn you to stay out of our business..... paid a visit to a certain bereft lady, eh?"

Biffy sharply took a breath as she read on

"Little girls don't snoop around finding clues. So aah... Trips... you are detectives uh?'

Biffy sank back inhaling heavily.

"Talking of clues, unravel this one: So close yet so far!"

Biffy controlled her breathing.

"Click...click...click!" behind her someone else tapped computer keys.

Biffy held her breath. Someone else was in the Centre with her...was it the same person messaging? Very quietly, after a brief introspection, Biffy got up and began to check the cubicles lined up in a row. Six cubicles, six computers.....

No...no...no..no...Biffy muttered in her mind as she peeped into four cubicles... no one there...the last one now...Biffy peeped in and...*no one!*

"Srrrummmm"

Biffy hastily turned and in dismay saw the exit door behind her silently begin to shut!

"Sniff-sniff" Biffy wrinkled her nose and exclaimed,

"*Lavender*...the same smell like in Mr Kalra's office that day... oh dear...was it the kidnapper....a female who wears lavender perfume...?!"

Yes, Biffy sniffed the strong smell of lavender that filled the air! Her legs propelled her towards the exit. *"Oh no, too late!"* Biffy exclaimed in frustration!

Staring at the slow motion shutting door, Biffy muttered, *"Someone has just left!* Was it the same person with lavender perfume?" Biffy rushed out but was confronted only by an empty corridor! "Ohhh, someone was there, someone I suspect was sending me those chat mails...I was so busy checking the cubicles that I missed the exit... drat!" Biffy groaned! The smell too dissipated as she reached the corridors since like the lobby room air fresheners, the smell of lemon, was the obvious fragrance.

Eleven

The next day, early in the morning to beat the heat, was sight-seeing day. Mama, along with Malti, took them to Chandni Chowk in an air-conditioned tourist taxi .

"Yummmy!" Piffy slurped the "jalebis" they were eating at a roadside kiosk. They all jammed into a shady spot, giggling and obviously having great fun being together.

"I need to buy some traditional trimmings and borders for my salwar kameez", Mama informed everyone generally. "This place is popular for all that!"

Biffy jingled her hands and feet. Mama had picked up traditional bangles as well as "payals" (anklets) for them. After this, they would be visiting the famous Jama Masjid.

The day, though a bright sunny one, hardly affected the family! Sweating it outdoors seemed to add to their adventure quotient. They were back at the hotel by noon. Mama retired to her room and the girls decided to watch television. Biffy was, as usual, restless. She drank cold water...bit into some fruit.... ....then finally decided to go up to the Business Centre. It was a quiet afternoon and the Centre had a deserted look. Biffy did not sit at the computer, instead she sat at the Reading Centre and read a Sherlock Homes mystery book. Soon, she dozed off.

"Scuffle.....thud.....wang!" Biffy's eyes flew open.

What were these sounds? Rubbing her eyes, she sat up. Biffy was nicely camouflaged by the huge arm of the single sofa she was sitting on. Creeping out, Biffy slowly opened the door and crept into

the isolated corridor. The sounds are coming from room 301....
hmmmm.....sounds like a drill... may be maintenance is working !

Just as Biffy put her ear to the door of 301, Malti's voice
interrupted her, "Biffy...I was looking all over for you...come on,
it's time to rest and not wander about." The sounds at 301 stilled
abruptly. Biffy had no choice but to leave with Malti.

And the strangest of sounds...!" Biffy was relating her experience
to her sisters in the evening when Mr Lal walked in, looking a bit
peeved.

"Can you believe it, *there has been a theft again*. Room 301 ...
an entire teak wood bed has been stolen piece by piece...this bed
was brought from a heritage fair....!"

Biffy's eyes widened, "the drill!" Miffy and Piffy made eye contact
but Papa Lal was saying, "Before we came, seems lots of things kept
being missed. But they were easily replaceable—mostly copper
kitchen utensils and books and magazine from the library! I feel
there is almost a pattern here, first the kitchen 101, then 201 now
301, that includes the Business Centre too! The security has made
it clear they are closely watching 401!"

"401? But...?" Mrs Lal looked puzzled and Mr Lal burst out
laughing.

"Yes, there is *no room* 401... just joking!" Mr Lal sobered and
said in a serious voice, "This whole disappearance of Mr Kalra is
shocking....hope we get some clue....!"

Biffy asked her father, "What has been stolen so far from these
rooms? Is the kidnapping connected..?"

"Aha, my detective daughter... this is not your league....this is Delhi,
let the hotel security solve this one!" Papa Lal chuckled, amused.

"Aw, Papa, tell me!"

Laughingly, Mr Lal indulged his daughter.

"I can see a pattern here!" Biffy, Piffy and Miffy sat in a private
enclosure in the lobby discussing the mystery. A police inspector
along with an ACP had just left after talking to the hotel staff. No

news on the Kalra front though!

Biffy, armed with paper and pen, wrote down the numbers of rooms of the burglaries. "First, it was 101…..then 201, now 301. Why these rooms? What I need to go over is what is being stolen… hmm… first an expensive copper planter…then an entire book and magazine collection from the Business Centre…two iron pots from the kitchen…now a bed! What a cheap-skate thief."

"How odd?"

"How shameless are the robbers…they are not scared at all!"

"How do they take all the stolen goods out?"

"Yes….what about the money stolen… is it all connected?"

Next day, commotion prevailed at the offices of the hotel.

"Save him……waaah…..sob sob!" Young Mrs Kalra sat in the manager's office and wept. Distraught, she showed them a letter dropped in her mail box.

Someone had cut out letters of the alphabet from magazines, and pasted them on a notebook's lined paper to form a message that said:

"Mrs Kalra go hotel
 Meet manager
 manager give Rs…… V release him…or he dead… give
 you 4 days! No police—inform, we will kill him."

"That sum is astronomical! This is serious. We have to call in the police," Mr Lal said.

Earlier, unable to handle a hysterical Mrs Kalra, the manager, Mr Sud, had requested Mr Lal to come to his office.

"No!" Mrs Kalra jumped up wringing her hands, her pretty face contorted in despair, "No please, no police…t-they w-ill kill him…sob"

"No, Sir. …I agree with her….Please. Think of the hotel reputation! I will think of some way to handle this…"

Mr Lal knew this was out of his jurisdiction, so he just shrugged.

Mr Sud patted Mrs Kalra and went to the phone. He spoke to Detective RK from the the hotel's security and told him to report to him immediately.

Events were unfolding rapidly......

"Little girl....so have you discovered the thief? Or the kidnapper?"

This message popped up again on Biffy's chat account. This time, Piffy and Miffy were sitting at the Business Centre computer along with Biffy.

"(gasp) Biffs, who is that?" Piffy exclaimed.

"Dunno!" Biffy sat back and mused, "Should I report this?"

"Yeah, I guess so...how has this...this whoever... got into your mail account?"

Biffy settled back further to think.

Sighing, she said in a firm voice: "No, I am not going to report this and be a 'namby- pamby' detective." Her sister groaned and she hissed, "Listen I am going to draw this ...blackmailer, whatever, out!"

"Ssssh...."Piffy, took a sharp breath, crying in warning, "Miffy-Biffy, that is so dangerous!"

"Hey, who is this?" Biffy typed, ignoring all calls of warnings.

"Now, wouldn't you want to know?" came the prompt reply.

"Of course....I am sure you want to know more about the discovery I have made....that can get whoever is involved into a lot of trouble."

Biffy furiously typed the above reply.

A pause from the other side, then : "Stop pretending you know something...you do not....I am not that dumb!"

Biffy wrote back...

"Ho ho ....OK....when I do tell my father, and the police my discovery, we will see who is pretending!"

There was no reply after that. The girls waited but in vain.

"Let's go..... it is late in the morning... we have lots to do!" Biffy finally said and the girls left.

Twelve

Mr Sud grimly stared at Detective RK. The ransom note that Mrs Kalra had given him lay open on the desk.

"Should we inform the police?" Mr Sud asked, glancing at the note.

"Nah...I am confident...I will trace them!" RK loftily claimed.

Incidentally, Mr Lal was present too. He shook his head but said nothing

Later, at dinner, however, Mr Lal, grumbled to the family.

"What?" Biffy jumped up and down on her chair.

"Papa, a ransom for Mr Kalra?!?"

"Yes." Mr Lal then described the cut out letters.

"Papa, *tell* the police....this is someone's life!" Biffy beseeched whilst her sisters nodded vigorously.

"I wish I could...though the police is on to the case, but a ransom makes it little complicated.. Sud is sure we can trace the kidnappers! And with this heroic deed, tell the police... this way he looks good in front of the bosses and the reputation of the hotel is safe! Moreover, Mrs Kalra is adamant! She says they, the kidnappers, will kill Mr Kalra, if we inform the police."

"Poor, poor lady!"

Biffy then asked, "Papa, where is the note?"

Papa was about to say something, then he closed his mouth, "Biffy, stay out of this! It is a grown-ups' job!" *"Aw Papa?!?"*

Mr Lal, however, refused to say anything.

"I am going to see if I can get the note!" Biffy said to Piffy and Miffy at bedtime.

"But why?" Piffy reproached

Biffy, as usual, ignored her, and turning to Miffy, she said, "Let us sneak out....we check the offices....may be the note will be lying around."

"Whose office?"

"See Manager Sud does not sit in Mr Kalra's office... I guess he is spooked out. But he sits in the introductory room that leads to the conference room, right?"

Miffy nodded.

"So let us go there and check things out right away."

"But Papa said a detective was on the case. May be that detective has taken the note?" Miffy surmised thoughtfully.

"You know, you may be right. But my hunch says the note may just be at Manager Sud's desk...let us check it all the same. I say!" Biffy decided.

Piffy refused to come with them. She raised her comforter cover over her face and lay inert. Rock, not bothered, slept peacefully. In the darkness, Miffy and Biffy groped their way out. They passed a snoring Malti.

"A ummmm!" Malti shifted and tossed, changing sides. The two girls froze. Biffy, in fact, had one foot in the air. She settled down and the two look alikes slowly opened the door... "Grrrrrrrrrr!" That was Rock reacting to *someone opening the door*! Luckily, Piffy now in a protective mode towards her sisters, scooped him up and put him under the comforter covers too! He, too, settled down!

The conference rooms were in the basement areas of the hotel. Right by the lifts by which the girls had descended sat a duty clerk! Seeing him, the two stopped abruptly.

"Hi!" he responded to the uncomfortable looking girls. Biffy was collecting her wits, wondering to how cross him and enter the conference room, so she gave him a vague smile!

His smile was wide and he said, "Up so late?"

"Um...hols are on...!" Before Biffy could say anything further, a service person dragged a cleaning contraption and wheeled it towards the conference rooms, from where Biffy was so desperately wanting to find clues!

"Boy, that vacuum cleaner is big!" Biffy giggled aloud even as her mind raced.

"Yes and extremely efficient!"

"Can I...we... go and watch how it functions?"

"Yes, why not!" The young duty manager would not dream of refusing the chef, Mr Lal's, daughters, this small request.

Heart singing, Biffy beckoned Miffy and they now very legally walked into the rooms. The staff boy or cleaner had started the vacuum cleaner and its hum filled the air.

Biffy immediately began an inspection around Mr Sud's desk. Miffy kept up a chatter to divert the staffer's attention. "Oh Miffeeee!" Biffy in a sing-song way called her sister a little later.

Miffy grinning at the preoccupied staffer, responded to her call nonchalantly, so as to not raise his suspicions. The staffer was not paying any attention actually, since he was plugging in the cleaner machine. Soon the vacuum cleaner noise drowned all sounds.

"Biffy, what?" Miffy gestured, surprised to see her sister sitting in a lotus position under Sud's desk. "See."

Biffy was holding the ransom note!

"Found in his desk drawer! The detective must have left it here for safekeeping. Surprisingly, the drawer was not locked!"

The security concerns of leaving such a vital clue as the ransom note in an unlocked drawer were lost as the girls eagerly inspected the note.

Biffy's mind worked furiously but she really could not come up with any clues! Biffy raised the note to her nose and took a deep breath, mumbling, "This note smells so nice...familiar smell....where... where, where....?" Biffy said holding the paper to her nose.

"Lavender....who wears lavender...is Kalra's 'nabber' a female...?!"

"Could be the gum smelling?" Miffy whispered.

"Nah...this is proper perfume...can't seem to think... is it an after shave...hmmmm? Omigosh...remember when I had sneaked into Mr Kalra's office...when I suspected he was up to something?"

Miffy rapidly nodded.

"Some female had come in...the one who never exited?"

"Hmm huh huh!" Miffy impatiently agreed.

"Well then, too, there was this smell of lavender! Same smell here too! I can swear it...then at the Business Centre, same smell.....!"

"Gasp... his kidnapper is a female?!"

"May be or she is an accomplice.....now, who could it be?"

But Biffy just could not recollect anything.

Frustrated, she returned the note to the drawer and hoisted herself up. Miffy too jumped up. Hailing a "thank you" to both the staffers, the two sisters returned to the lobby and made their way to their room.

The following day at the lobby......

"Hello little girls...what is happening?" Shweta straddling her laptop under her arm came towards the Trips, smiling. They were sitting in the lobby putting the events together.

"So Shweta Didi, have they found Mr Kalra?" Miffy asked. "Poor Mr Kalra...no...no news.....disappearing from the garden patch is odd and a ransom note even odder, if there is such a word!"

"Yes, very.....but how come the police is also at a loss?"

"Smart kidnappers, I guess...police apparently is being outsmarted!"

"Ooops!" Shweta dropped her hanky and giving out a full throated laugh, she bent to pick it up. Smiling, she lifted her hanky and waved a bye.

"She is so happy he is gone," whispered Piffy after Shweta was walking away.

"I would be.....he was so nasty to her." Miffy agreed.

Biffy suddenly sat up as if she had been electrified. She sat staring beyond the departing Shewta as if she had seen something! "Biffy... what happened?" her sisters cried. Biffy just shook her head.

It was apparent she was trying to gather her wits!

"Is Shweta in danger?"

But Biffy snapped, "Let me think...unravel...let's go...!"

"Um- sorry....are these taken...oh, it is the Trips, right?" A voice interrupted them.

Gulping hard and collecting her wits, Biffy looked up. The voice belonged to Mrs Kalra.

Mrs Kalra, with a tired sigh, sat down next to them.

The girls stared at her. She was looking stunning in a long skirt complemented by a tight blouse and on her feet were smart boots. Her hair was styled to be wavy, left loose. Biffy gave her a 'your husband has been kidnapped, where do get the time to be so dressy?' look.

Mrs Kalra settled her big designer bag on the lounge chair and said, "What is up?"

"What is up with you?" Biffy bluntly asked much to the consternation of her sisters. They thought Biffy was very rude indeed!

But Mrs Kalra did not seem to mind. She answered prettily, moving her hands up and down, "I... I... oh dear, things are getting worse....I don't know what is happening.....this kidnapping...no clues...!" She made a sad face. Biffy restlessly narrowed her eyes and stared at her.

Miffy noticed this and she nudged Biffy. Instead of backing off, suddenly Biffy lunged forward. Completely taken aback, Mrs Kalra shrank back with a shocked whimper. Biffy went up very close to Mrs Kalra'a neck took a deep breath! Then Biffy, with a smile, shrugged her shoulders and said, "Thanks!"

The awkward silence that followed was certainly uncomfortable!

"Let us go!" Biffy addressed her sisters. With a nod, the Trips said their byes. Mrs Kalra, looking slightly shaken by Biffy unexpected behaviour, nodded uneasily.

"What was that?" Piffy furiously demanded. Miffy put in a strong, "Yeah, what was that??" They stood at the lift doors.

"Nothing, just smelling for lavender….!" Biffy drawled

"*Biffy…that is no way* ….er.. but, tell us, was she …?"

"What?" Biffy asked as they entered the lift which had come.

"Smelling of lavender?"

Her answer was lost as the lift door closed, taking them up to their room!

Shweta had no idea she was in any kind of danger or that she was being spied on. Dangerously close were her spies, though extremely discreet! She went about her work and tasks totally unaware! If she was at the desk, she was watched; in the lobby, watched; at the porch, watched; even in the gardens, watched!

When Shweta came up directly to room 101 ostensibly to call the house-keeper, she still had no idea the corridor accommodated her spy too! It was six o' clock in the morning and not many guests were up yet!

She traipsed with muffled footfalls on the carpet and silently used the master keys to let herself into the room.

The spy followed her undetected inside too.

Shweta seemed oblivious of another presence. She was well into the room where an old fashioned dressing table stood.

Shweta did something very odd… she pushed the entire dressing table and mirror…the dresser was conveniently on wheels as in most hotels, to make cleaning easier. A door presented itself behind the dressing table. Shweta unlocked the door and slipped inside, leaving the door wide open.

The spy followed her too. Peeping into the door, the spy discovered a service stairway. Gingerly stepping into the open doorway, the spy never saw the sack coming......... the sack went over her head and then her hands were bound tightly.

"Help! Ouch! Let go!" Biffy, er... the *spy*... yelped but nobody seemed to hear her. Her "grabber" pushed her, blindfolded by the sack, down the stairs.

Piffy and Miffy were getting worried. Biffy had gone in after Shweta and had not come out. Using sign language, she had earlier asked them to station themselves in any hiding place around the corridor; which they had. They even saw Biffy slip in behind Shweta.

Relieved, they heard the door knob of 101 turn. Shweta stepped out, humming gaily under her breath. *Biffy was not there!*

Where was Biffy?

Locking the door, Shweta walked down the corridors once again. From where Miffy was hidden, she could clearly see Shweta. Piffy could not. Piffy was hidden in one corner, and its angles made it impossible to peep out! However, Miffy could make eye contact with Piffy . Miffy gesticulated that she was going to check on Biffy. Piffy nodded, beseeching with her eyes for her hurry back! Miffy nodded. Leaving her own hiding place and beckoning to Piffy to stay where she was, Miffy followed Shweta and disappeared down the corridor. Piffy, still hidden, waited impatiently. "Where was Miffy?" Piffy was not brave. She sat hidden for the longest time, then gathered courage to have a peek!

When Piffy peeped out, *she saw Shweta!*

Standing, in the middle of the corridor, uncertainly.

Where was Miffy?

This thought drove Piffy out of her hiding place and she ran to Shweta.

"Hello Didi!" Piffy called.

"Why the er… one of the Trips…?"

Piffy panted to a stop in front of Shewta.

"Where are the others?"

"Didi …we…I.. er…"

"Oh I know where they are. Do you want to find them too?"

Piffy nodded dumbly. "Come," Shweta beckoned, returning to room 101.

Sigh! Piffy in the next ten minutes found herself suddenly with her head in a sack and bundled off in the same manner as Biffy and Miffy!

How come the Trips were trailing Shweta?

Simple.

It all happened the previous day! Remember, when Biffy, Piffy and Miffy were correlating the incidents? In the lobby, where they had met Shweta too? Suddenly, Biffy had turned strange and shaken? Now, there was a reason why Biffy had been so shaken. Shweta, when she bent to pick up her hanky, came close to Biffy; *Biffy had caught the strong fragrance of lavender emitting from her!* Moreover, another thought that tore into Biffy's mind simultaneously then was something Shweta had said! The smell of lavender and the thought bounced into her mind all together! You see, she remembered Shweta saying: "Mr. Kalra had been nabbed from the garden patch." *No one ever said that!* As far as the story went, he had disappeared, period !Also, Shweta, mentioning the ransom note…no one except Papa, Mr Sud and the detective knew about the note! So the needle of suspicion naturally pointed at Shweta! That is how the 'trail Shweta' plans began! Their suspicions got strengthened when they followed Shweta around and saw her habitually spraying pocket lavender perfume on her wrists time and again! Biffy had then remarked, "So Shweta has a fetish for spraying perfume! She must have sprayed the ransom note too."

But now Shweta had got the better of them. She had kidnapped them effectively. The Trips had disappeared from the 1st floor of the hotel and no one was the wiser!

"Where are the girls?" Malti pressed her hands worriedly and paced the hotel room. Rock sat sadly, head down, by the door. He too was waiting for the girls. Mrs Lal was away for an early morning flower show at the main hotel.

Malti was upset. Mrs Lal had left very early. The girls were still sleeping. Malti had gone out to pick up bread from the pastry shop and when she returned, the room, save for Rock, was empty!

They are not in their bed or the gardens, where have they disappeared early in the morning? Should I inform Sir-Madam? Oh no, may be not..the Trips do take off at times…may be they are at the Business Centre…but I cannot go there ….only the key card can be swiped for entry…oh dear…..." Malti paced the room in a fretful fuss.

Meanwhile, Mr Sud panicked when a ransom call came to him in the conference room. He rushed blindly to the kitchens.

"A ransom call has come …..in the conference room!" The harried manager rushed into kitchen area and in a fierce, private whisper, informed Mr Lal. "The caller specifically asked for you Mr Lal," Mr Sud further provided.

"Me? But why", puzzled, Mr Lal asked. But all the same, he walked forward and calmly nodded to the chef trainees to continue icing the Canadian frizzy chocolate cake he was demonstrating as part of his capsule. He then followed the manger to the conference room.

"We are on video conferencing. He will redial again….so wait.. this guy is smart…he called us here…to the conference room… does not speak more than two minutes so we cannot trace the call immediately…" the manager spoke almost in a jabber to Mr. Lal.

"Who will be calling….?" Mr Lal mumbled and the answer came soon enough….

"Welcome, Mr Lal," boomed a voice.

On the conference room screen via web video camera, a

shadowy silhouette graced the screen. Obviously, the kidnapper was protecting his own identity... neither Mr Lal or Mr Sud could make out who was on the screen!

"I have your daughters... all three.. how much ransom are you willing to pay? Must I add, when it was a poor hotel employee...er Mr Kalra...you dithered and no ransom was paid...now what are you giving for all of them, eh?"

The Trips, confused and yelling, suddenly illuminated the screen, then "Click" the phone was off!

Mr Lal gripped the chair handle and his face went white.

Let us see what was happening with the Trips. For that, we have to go to a remote room in the deep environs of the hotel.

"Where are we?" Miffy hissed to Biffy.

Piffy said in a scared voice (sob), "The ropes tying my hands hurt".

Biffy inspected her surroundings.. "What a small room this is... hmm no window....only a skylight.....hmmmm. Seems like part of the room has gone there.. may be when the hotel was renovated...." Biffy indicated to beyond one wall. "This half remains. See the walls are quite fancy...sculpted and..."

"Biffy...listen, can you imagine!" Miffy interrupted her, "It was Shweta all the time...She is strong...how she sacked and tied us..."

"Yes...smart cookie though.. one by one she trapped us... what a fool I have been!" Biffy grumbled.

"You and your bright ideas...gosh, this is the end!" Piffy wailed.

The Trips were sitting in the centre of the small room, back to back, hands bound, but head sacks off. Shweta, to be doubly sure, had tied their waists together with rope too!

So here were the Trips, hands bound, back to back, and strapped even further by a waist strap! They had not seen anyone. So when Shweta handling a camera suddenly opened the door, the Trips simultaneously yelled *"Let us go..what do you want?"*

Shweta shrugged, ignoring them. After filming, she left, locking the door of the room with a loud click.

A dismal silence followed the click.

Biffy mulishly stuck her underlip out. "Now listen....I have a plan!"

Her sisters listened carefully... but gasped, "You have gone mad! It will never work."

In the conference room, more chaos was unfolding!

"Bring a glass of water, quick" the manager shouted as Mr Lal, though not unconscious but very shocked, slumped on the chair. Meanwhile, Mrs Lal, yes *Mrs Lal*, rushed into the conference room too!

"Bring two glasses of water!" The manager had to shout two minutes later. Mrs Lal, on hearing what had happened, sank, with a long wail!

How was Mrs Lal there too?

Actually, earlier Mrs Lal came looking for Mr Lal in the kitchens. She had enjoyed herself at the flower show. On her return to the hotel, she needed to speak to her husband. On hearing that he was in the conference room, she had just casually peeked in to see if he could talk. She needed some bank details, you see. That is where she chanced to hear about the kidnapping!

"How did this happen?", presently, croaked Mrs Lal.

"Hush...we will figure something out," Mr Lal, collecting his wits, managed to mumble.

In the remote room, in another part of the hotel, Biffy seemingly was taking charge, even though tied hand and foot!

"Now at the count of three...jump and move!" Biffy instructed her sisters. Tied back to back, waists attached, the three were attempting a ridiculous manoeuvre so it seemed! But Biffy had full confidence she would get this plan/idea of hers through!

"The idiot Shweta who tied us, failed to tie our feet. Admitted she tied our hands and waists very tightly. So now we attempt to stand up first!" Biffy mumbled, scrabbling her feet up so as to stand.

"One...two..three, up!"

Piffy delayed at the "up" so the measures kind of failed... you know, to stand up together.

"Again...one two upppp! Phew!" And with a sigh of relief, they were all three standing upright. That is when she gritted, "Now at the count of three...jump and move!" "Oof...ooow...stop... stamping my foot!" was the symphony of words that interrupted this orchestrated negotiation towards the door. *"jump.....step up....draggggggggg....stop pulling to the left...aaargh....stop...now move...move...jumpppppp!"*

Finally, the shut door was reached.

"Sit!" Biffy ordered. The three hit the ground together.

"Ow...that hurt...my bound hands are killing me!" Piffy wailed.

"Ssssssh! Miffy you press the back of your head near my mouth.

Piffy muttered, "You and your stupid ideas...!"

Miffy and Biffy ignored her. Throwing up her head so it was closer to Biffy's mouth, Miffy sat still. Biffy too pressed her head close to Miffy head. To an observer this whole exercise might appear foolish and difficult but Biffy was clear about what she intended to do. Pouting her lips and grabbing with her teeth, Biffy slowly began to remove a hair pin *from Miffy's head!*

"Don't move Miffy....."

"Ouch you are pulling my hair!"

"Got it!" Biffy triumphantly dropped the pin on her side but was given no time for further actions.

Footfalls filled the air from the other side of the door.

"Someone is coming!"

All exercise stopped and in the nick of the seconds that followed the footfalls coming closer towards the door, the girls dragged themselves, sat jumped and scrambled back to where they were originally sitting. They barely managed to settle back when the door opened.

It was Shweta and Mrs Kalra!!!! Yes, Mrs Kalra, in sneakers, blow dried hair and a jazzy sweat shirt and tracks!

Shweta grimly whispered, "Stupid girls, why could you not keep your nose out of our business?"

"So what did you think? That she could tie you up on her own huh?" Mrs Kalra rudely addressed a shocked Piffy who was confusedly staring at her.

"But it is your husband who is kidnapped..." Biffy demanded.

"So what, eh? I need the bucks...my...er...life-style demands big money...you children are the pits, spoiling my plans....grrrr!" Mrs Kalra contorted her features and spat out. She then turned and said to Shweta, "I am leaving...take care!" Mrs Kalra then nonchalantly exited.

"So, what do you think? Smart, are we not?" Shweta preened to the Trips!

Getting no appropriate reply except some unprintable mutters from Biffy, Shweta said, "I need to gag you girls! Er...I would have head sacked you...but you can still scream through the sacks... moreover, I need the sacks to fill goods....sacks were fine to confuse you enough for us to tie you up...but now...er...so um... so gagging it is....Master scolded me...all because of you stupid girls..why can't keep your nose out of our business...I have to gag you!" She decided firmly.

Biffy yelled, "halp...halp" and kicked and strained at the ropes. This was a cue for the others and they screamed too!

"HALP...HELP....HARRRRRRLP....AAAAAAHAHAHHH HELP!"

Shweta startled, shushed them in panic, "hush...hush....ohhhh.... sssshhhh!" Then she ran around the room and came back with a stout stick....that stick looked suspiciously like the leg of a bed!

It was then that the Trips noted the pile of the dismantled bed stacked against the wall!

Shweta using the bed leg (held in both her hands), from the back, angled Biffy's neck in a strangler's hold!

"Cough…choke…spat….aaaaaagh!" Biffy choked!

Her sisters were shocked into silence. Tied as they were, it was impossible to fight back!

When she let Biffy go, Biffy was dizzy and out of sorts. It was a cakewalk for Shweta to gag them after that. To her credit, she did wait for Biffy to get her breath back before she gagged her too.

She proceeded to stuff hankies in their mouths and then duck taped them. She surveyed her handiwork and then, as if remembering something, exclaimed, "Um, silly me, I think I need to tie your feet too…um…but where is the rope? Um we ran out of rope… my Master will kill me if I go back and tell him! First, I forgot to duck tape….then got less rope…shucks….. moreover, he wants me nowhere near this place till the morning……..!" Shweta stood musing seriously aloud. Shaking her head, she glanced at the wide-eyed, gagged girls, listening to her inane discussion with herself, and shrugged, "Please, it is not my custom to choke little girls with bed legs…see, now you have upset me (sob)." Shweta actually sniffed, pulled out a tiny bottle of perfume spray, and puffed some on her wrists. She raised her left wrist to her nose and closed her eyes, taking a deep breath. Then she raised her right wrist and took another deep breath.

The girls now quite believed they were dealing with a weirdo! Shweta, obviously composing herself, said, "With the door locked there is no way you can escape ..not so smart, eh? Now you cannot holler"…. Then more menacingly, "Don't even try any tricks, got it?"

She was out of the room.

Biffy and her sisters sat in complete silence for a while. They all had one thought though… how could Mrs Kalra betray her husband this way!?! Poor, poor Mr Kalra! Horrid wife he had! She must be working with the others too. What a shady lady she turned out to be!

Ultimately, Biffy's eyes wandered around the room.

Then Biffy yelped, "IUmhgh gn-ot it-H!" He voice odd since her mouth was gagged. Translated it meant: "I got it!"

"Ummmghn....!" (come) Biffy indicated they continue with her plan.

"Howwwwng?" That is Miffy asking how.

"Cmnhhghhh!(come)" Biffy urged them towards the left wall. Piffy and Biffy thinking she was quite mad, grunted and protesting, followed. As soon as Biffy reached the wall, she dragged her face sideways to make contact with the plaster of Paris (POP) beading sculpted in a wave through the middle of the left wall! Stretching, Biffy began scraping the edge of the duck tape covering her mouth against the rough sculpting! Squeezing in her cheeks, so that the tape lost grip, Biffy, in spite of the extreme discomfort the others were in, scraped the tape over the coarse edges. The duck tape, not of very good quality, began to give! Rolling it by using the irregular surface, Biffy pushed it from her mouth. Tugging, pouting, moving her jaws and lips, Biffy finally got the tape off her mouth. "Pstttooo!" she spat out the gag. The duck tape hung to one side, rolled and sticky! A black sticky residue of duck gum circled the area around her mouth!

"Gasp...your turn now!"

Painstakingly the other two removed the tape similarly!

Considered an ornamental design, the scalloped edging to beautify the wall came as a blessing, so it seemed!

"So how does this help!" Miffy asked once the gag was spat out.

"Hush ..look for the pin!" That proved very arduous but eventually the hairpin from Miffy's head was found.

"Miffy, pick the pin with your teeth first."

Miffy, now with growing respect for her sister, complied quickly. Almost heaving the two on her back, she bent forward and tried to lick up the fallen pin!

"Uffffffnggggggggg!" Her teeth hit the dirty floor...hating it. Miffy, however, managed to pick up the pin. Her expressions at scooping up dust along with the pin were classic but Biffy was ignoring that.

"Try to put it on my shoulder straight, Miffs ol girl, now!"

Twisting her head and trying to make sure the flat long thin hair pin was safely placed on Biffy's shoulders, Miffy completed the exercise.

Biffy with full concentration lifted the hairpin from Miffy's shoulders with her mouth. All that twisting and stretching hurt but Biffy was concentrating fully on the task in hand! Piffy whined.."My hands are hurting...what is all this.." But her wails were disregarded.

Biffy now shifted amongst minor protests from her tied-up sisters to directly face the door and the key hole.

"Using her teeth Biffy straightened the pin and gripped it with her teeth. Now she carefully adjusted the pin into the keyhole; pushed in the hair pin and..... ....

"creaaaakkkkk...... smmmrgh." *Effortlessly the door opened!.*

An astounded silence followed at such early success! Thoughts of slipping hair pins and unsuccessful attempts at unlocking the click lock were put to rest. You know why? Because Shweta in her foolish absentmindedness had *forgotten to fully close the door* when she had left! Upset at having to deal with three screaming girls who protested at being gagged, and made her, Shweta, look so bad, was all that rambled in her mind! So on her way out, she forgot to shut the door properly!

As of now, even the Trips never guessed this and totally believed the hair pin trick was a success!

Piffy and Miffy were dumbfounded at Biffy's smartness!

"Uggggnggggggggh" Biffy moved forwards and tried to kick the door wider open......"Stand up all at once. One ..two umggggh THREE!"

Trips jumped up and Biffy kicked open the door wider!

"Careful, this a click lock, so if it closes, it will lock!" Biffy warned, pushing into the doorway fast.

"Yew stop pulling...eow my hands...come...yeoch!' came three different responses all at once!

"Gasp, it is the same stairway from room 101..." Biffy indicated over and behind her shoulder on top, then forward in front to a door down below the small flight of steps!

Yes, they had been kidnapped and kept in an actual hotel room that had been divided when the renovations took place! One part of the room went into the hotel area to make up a fancy toilet area, and the other part that had recently accommodated the Trips, lay forgotten on this side! Nestled between floors at the service stairways of the hotel, no one could have guessed a room was there!

"Biffy..... um one-two –three-four five six...stairs to trundle down, *we can fall head first Biffs!*" Miffy warningly pointed out, showing her the steps to go down and reach the door!"

"*But we have too!*" Biffy firmly said.

Resigned the other two, hands bound backwards with their determined sister edged forward. Mastermind Biffy led them first to the top of the stairs.

"I move, then you step down with me!" Biffy said.

"Ahhhh slowly........ EOW MY HANDS!" came Piffy, voice intermingled again.

They moved to the first step...second step...third...fourth... off stumbled, then balanced on the fifth...finally, the sixth step, and home!

Thirteen

"Oh gosh………the door is locked!" Miffy cried. When they came down all struggling, bent and venturing carefully, Miffy happened to face the door this time!

"Really?..Let me see." So exercise jump together to turn followed. When Biffy was facing the door, she too muttered angrily, "Drat locked!"

"I-t-think that is…" Piffy muttered.

"Piffy, I am sick of your complaining. I got you till here did I not?!" Biffy snarled.

"Biffs….I think…"

"Piffy just clam up….!"Miffy also snapped irritated.

"Listen you two…there is a key!" Piffy raised her voice to snap back!

"What?"

Ye-s…hanging on a nail on the opposite wall…see." True enough, Piffy was facing the wall where a key hung by a nail!

So jump around together began and Biffy let out a chuckle, "Yes, so there is!" They hopped and jumped towards the key!

"Ungggg….it is too high….c-antttt stretch so high… unggggggg!"

Frustrated, the three stared at the key hanging higher then they could comfortably reach with hands bound backwards!

"OK…no giving up. Come, jump to stand directly under the key..come on…ooof stop pushing!" Biffy moved and said.

They were under the key.

"Jump as high as you can….one-two-threeeeee!" Biffy facing the wall with the key, jutted her chin out and banged at the edge of the key to dislodge it. The whole process failed. Biffy scraped her chin though.

"OK, once again…one two three-eeee!"

Tut tut, failed again. Dismally, the three stood in frustrated silence.

"This is silly…..forget it…let's go …!"

Painfully trying not to cry out since her scraped chin hurt badly, her sister could not see that….Biffy sternly said, "One last time.. then I'll think up of something else.

One---two …three-eeeee!"

Fourteen

Shweta timidly lowered her eyes then lifted them wide-eyed at the hotel security detective and made sure her voice stammered, "T-this is a-all so shocking....the alarm...all this?"

The detective from the main security agency was called RK. He found her quite pretty and appreciatively gave her a once over and softened his voice to say, "Of course, you are shocked...please... take your time...tell me who do you suspect, you know, about the kidnapping of Kalra."

Shweta once again gave the innocent wide-eyed look, "M-me.... suspect someone...oh no! But please...Mr Kalra kidnapped...now the girls...oh dear!"

RK straightened abruptly. He had been bending over the reception desk you see! He narrowed his eyes and asked suspiciously, "Girls? Which girls are kidnapped...I know nothing about girls?"

Shweta went white, ruffled, she clicked on the keys on her desk computer, then cleared her throat to say, "Girls...no, I said poor me as in me girl...me..er..girl...has to deal with such... um... fright...no girls are kidnapped...it is *me* er *the girl* who is scared...!" Shweta convincingly said.

All the playacting caught the detective's heart. He could not possibly doubt this innocent young gir!

He gently patted her hand and consoled, "Oh such fear... worry not....I misunderstood...don't worry, I will do all to find the culprits....you relax...I will take care!"

"Oh you will? You are so brave…imagine a *detective*…!"

RK swelled with vain pride. Thinking his expression was very buccaneer and rakish, he repeated, "Don't worry..I…ahem…the detective…will get this all sorted..!"

Hiding the smile in her lowered eyes, Shweta timorously nodded, though her heart was beating rapidly.

When the detective walked away from the reception, he muttered to his fellow companion, "Poor thing…not at all involved! I know. Ten years in this detective business, I can read people….so she is not a suspect!"

His companion nodded, believing his senior completely.

The lobby area was bustling and no evidence of the crisis in the conference room had surfaced yet! Shweta was a bundle of nerves—her earlier gaffe with the detective had unsettled her!

The phone at her side rang, "Good morning front desk…this is Shweta how may… I help you?" Shweta said into the phone.

A silence.. then a squeaky voice said, "Hello…hello…I call from Mumbai…I am Mr Lal's mother……want to speak to my son Mr Lal—he is the chef.."

Listening into the phone, Shweta's mind switched lanes to more humorous paths as she thought, ho ho Mr Lal's mother? Um interesting….I will connect you to the conference room Maji… ha… ha tut tut as of now your son is so busy….Mr Lal is searching for something you see.. his lost daughters actually! Shweta was so deep in her thoughts and it was only the persistent, "Hello, hello!" on the phone that startled her out of her reverie!

Yes, Shweta suddenly sobered and said in a serious automated voice, "Good morning to you… I will transfer the call….. !"

Shweta, so preoccupied with her own bubbling evil thoughts plus the unnerving episode with the detective, clicked buttons unthinkingly. What she failed to realised was how an outstation call was coming in from the hotel's internal phone.

When the phone rang in the conference room, Mr Lal standing

next to the phone immediately whipped up the phone. Expressions changing in a million ways over his face, Mr Lal heard the voice on the phone, then without a word, banged down the phone and ran out of the room mumbling, " Gotta go…stay here …I have to attend to some hotel business!'

Mrs Lal looked stunned. So did the manager. Mr Lal, in the middle of all this, wanted to return to work …how strange that was! Mr Lal was gone, leaving behind a very awkward silence indeed.

"Er…he is a workaholic …" Mrs Lal said apologetically.

The manager felt so bad for poor Mrs Lal..he nodded sympathetically. Poor lady had to really contend with a husband who put work before everything—literally!

When Mr Lal stealthily let himself into the first floor corridor, he was shocked to see Malti standing looking very perturbed. "I phoned you, Sir. The girls are safe! Sorry Sir, I pretended to be your Mother!(Gulp) I had crossed my fingers' hoping the receptionist did not realise my call is being made from the internal phone...I.."

"Malti…what?" Mr Lal impatiently snapped.

"Sir…I am so sorry…however….No one saw you I hope? Especially that Shweta?"

"No….though I felt strange behaving like a slinky spy but… anyhow you said that the children are safe?'

"Oh yes, they are Sir…" Malti hesitantly nodded.

"Where are they..the girls?

"That is a long story…..but first…." Malti raised a hand and "Bang crash---shatterrrrrrrr!" Malti using the pickaxe in the glass case, broke the fire alarm window! Mr Lal was astounded no doubt! "Clang clang clang." The alarm screamed. "Malti whaaaa?" Mr Lal gasped.

"Sir, return downstairs quick. Meet me after the hotel is completely empty at Mr Kalra's office….excuse me I still have something to do...!" Saying this, Malti rushed away, leaving behind a very flummoxed Mr Lal!

Fifteen

EARLIER......

"One...two..three-eeeeee!"

The Trips jumped.

Biffy crashed into the key with her chin and with a thump it fell off the nail and to the ground. Miffy quickly stalled its roll with her foot!

"Owwwww owww owwwww!" Biffy yelped. The nail had scraped her chin too.

Anyways, she calmed down, and another exercise to pick up the key began. Heaving the two on her back, Biffy now quite a pro, picked up the key. She grimaced at its metal taste! With her baggage of siblings she then confronted the key hole. Sighing, Biffy bent down to kneel and face the key hole.... "O ow.... Grunt... humph...errrr" so did Piffy and Miffy...facing the other way, of course! Two attempts failed to open the door.

Sheesh! A pin works better, thought Biffy, still under the impression that she had opened the *previous door with a pin!*.

OK, this time it will work! Firmly, Biffy inserted the key with her mouth. Gripping the key tightly with her teeth she turned the lock. "Click!" The door lock opened.

With a major effort, Biffy, using her scraped chin, opened the door handle!

Oh no! *A wooden wall covered the doorway.*

"I think this is a cupboard.. hopefully with wheels..to camouflage the door....like the dresser in 101. Silly, to get in Shweta and her gang too must be sliding it aside.. let's get to work!"

"Ughnn how do we remove it?" Piffy asked in despair.

"With our feet…mine, I mean…OK, station up tight."

The two sisters Piffy and Miffy bent forward and firmly pressed their feet down to steady themselves. Biffy using their backs, lifted both her feet and firmly planted them on the wooden surface facing her. Using her feet, she pushed the wooden wall as one would a sliding door. "Just as I thought, this one is on wheels too!" Biffy muttered,

In no time, the wooden wall shifted and an opening emerged.

Squeezing, pushing and shoving through the girls entered a room and all together yelped, *"Gasp…. Mr Kalra's office!"*

The plush carpeted office never looked so familiar. The place was isolated. The Trips stood near Kalra's desk, still very much tied up together.

Biffy cried, "We need a plan…we cannot expose ourselves…I hope that Shweta does not come …quick, think!"

Shweta would not come in just now. She had been warned to stay clear of Mr Kalra's office by her Master for some reason. So as of now, the Trips were quite safe! They, of course, did not know that. So their actions were very hurried and nervous!

"Think-think-think", Biffy muttered under her breath.

The three introspected and Biffy's eyes travelled all over the room and finally settled on the desk phone.

"Got it!"

Miffy and Piffy did not protest as Biffy hopped, jumped and struggled to the phone.

Using her chin, she dislodged the handset. It lay on the desk. Using the tip of her tongue she pressed three numbers. When someone said "Hello", the girls rejoiced. Biffy went closer to the phone lying on its side on the desk and into the phone mouthpiece said, "Malti Didi, we need you to…." Biffy voice lowered warningly to add… "Didi, very discreetly…"

Yes, Biffy had dialled their room directly, hoping against hope Malti would answer!

"Is that you Biffs? O my gosh ...where.."

"Didi, please listen, we are in trouble...come to Mr..."

"Trouble ...whaaa?"

"Didi!" Biffy boomed and then there was silence.

"Didi, very discreetly.. without the front desk suspecting.... please come to Mr Kalra's office...bring your big scissors and the fruit knife too!"

"*Biffy-eee!*" But Malti got no answers as the phone clicked off.

"Yeow....yech!" Biffy hated using her mouth and teeth to pick up the handset and dropping it on its place!

Malti nervously picked up the scissors and knife and left the room.

Getting past the front desk into the offices was easy since Shweta was busy with a hotel guest at one end of the counter. Malti gasped when she saw her charges to say the least!

Quickly, they were untied and freed with the help of the scissors and fruit knife.

Malti was livid on hearing how her charges were treated by Shweta.

Relieved to be free of their bonds, the girls moved/rubbed their arms, hands and wrists to get the blood circulation back.

"Ow...it hurts!" they exclaimed!

"Let's go...will tell Mr Lal...!" Malti made towards the door.

"No," Biffy almost raised her voice.

Malti, Piffy and Biffy turned shocked, "But why...let us go and expose her.....!" Miffy exclaimed.

"No. No we are not informing anyone just yet...." Biffy firmly said, "Shweta spoke of a Master....then Mr Kalra...if we catch Shweta who is a small fry...she will warn her Master and Mr Kalra may be in danger! Poor Mr Kalra kidnapped thus, adding to this, it is his own wife who is at the bottom of it all!"

"So, then, what do we do?"

"So we trap Shweta…!"

"How?"

"By stealing her laptop…!"

"What?"

"See, her laptop must be having some clue…she is constantly referring to it…I am sure, there will be a clue."

"So how do we get to her laptop? Then, even if we do, how do we open her account?"

"See, her account is always open and she is constantly chatting.. we know that don't we? She needs to leave the counter for at least twenty minutes to give me time to take a look. Didi, this is where you come in. You go to Shweta… somehow get her away from the counter…..how do we do that?"

"The fire alarm..everyone has to leave the hotel…..that gives me the time!"…"

"So who is going to set off the fire alarm?" Miffy asked almost innocently.

"Biffy gave Malti a long look!

"Preposterous… I will not set off any alarms, forget it!" Malti firmly announced, stretching out her words!

"Come, come, leave this childish madness, and let's go …" Malti dismissed the idea, moving and, signalling them to move too.

"Didi, please…this is a good deed—best deed—please help! And if you are not going to help us …then, sorry, we escape from the rooms and do it without you…you know there is no way you can keep me from doing that?"

Malti was a simple person…she knew Biffy could do anything she set her mind on. Malti thought for a while, then said, "All right, get the laptop…but then if you get nothing, I can report the matter?"

Biffy nodded vigourously.

"OK… Er how do I start the alarm?"

"Just go to any floor, look for the fire alarm… and with the provided pickaxe, break the small window and pull the lever.."

"Are you mad… that is a jailing offence… no I will not do it…?" Malti nervously interrupted. "Didi, please…at the end, it is for a good cause.. do it please..szzzzz! We need to save Mr Kalra….!" Biffy then explained in detail. Malti unable to refuse, stealthily left the room. But all the while she had decided she would somehow make contact with Mr Lal….. She did not want to concern Mrs Lal just yet…

After a good twenty minutes, there was a huge clanging and the uproar that Biffy wanted was created! Everyone began moving out of the hotel. Things were quite volatile in the conference room too!

After Mr Lal's sudden departure, further conversation was abruptly silenced by a sudden loud clanging.

CLANG CLANG CLANG!

Noise filled the room, startling everyone witless!

CLANG…CLANG CLANG….PRILLLLLLLLLLL!"

Aaaaargh….is that an alarm!" Mrs Lal burst out, covering her ears.

"CLANG CLANG CLANG!" Urgently the sound went.

Cursing under his breath, the manager gasped "It is the fire alarm…we need to leave the office."

"Oh no, could be a trap…er trick…!"

"We cannot stay, it is against rules…we need to get the guests out!" Mr Sud, taking Mrs Lal's elbow to guide her out, said.

"B-ut-but…!" Mrs Lal looked at the blank video conferencing screen and exclaimed, "He may be back..!"

"Come..later….please!" The manager hustled everyone out. Everyone was moving rapidly outdoors. Soon the fire engines came in with their blaring horns!

Shweta did not budge. She, of course, stood transfixed at the sudden clanging. She stared wide-eyed at the commotion the clanging had caused. But did not move!

Meanwhile, Malti who had done her job, ran down, holding Rock, and was crossing the lobby when she caught Biffy pressed against the office door and gesturing towards Shweta. Biffy aggressively signalled to Malti to do something to move Shweta away from the laptop!

Malti did not let her down. In a panicky voice, she ran around the the front desk, "Shweta Ma'am, have you seen the Trips? I cannot find them, come help me, come please, there is a fire alarm...oh dear." She pulled Shweta with one free hand. Shweta reluctant to leave the laptop, resisted, but she was nothing against Malti's planned persistence. Nodding and confused, Shweta left with Malti. Even as she tried to lift up the laptop to carry it with her, Malti managed to pull her away!

Rock yipped and yapped but could only struggle in Malti's arms.

Biffy ducked and cautiously ran under the counter. Her aim was to reach the laptop resting atop the counter! She stuck her head out for a second over the counter and...*A foreign female guest stared directly at her curiously!*

The guest was rushing out towards the entrance when her attention was deflected to Biffy!

Biffy dived for cover but the guest twittered, "Oh dear, there is a child under the counter!"

The hotel staff member who was ushering everyone out, came to her side and urged, "Ma'am please, we need to vacate the building.."

"But there is a child under the front desk counter!" She insisted almost in a reproachful voice.

"A child? OK. I will check, please Ma'am, please proceed to the entrance!"

Still glancing over her shoulder, the guest reluctantly left. Meanwhile, the staffer stretched full on his heels to look over the counter. "No one! I think I will go around and check…"

"Hey….listen…hey hotel bellhop…hey come here!" Another hotel guest, putting his head through the entrance door, called suddenly, hailing the staffer.

Glancing at the counter, then at the calling guest, the staffer shrugged and immediately rushed towards the guest. "Hey staffer, I left my…" complained the guest indignantly. The usher comforted the guest and guided him out.

Now the hotel was absolutely empty, and the clanging had stopped.

Where was Biffy?

Tightly squeezed beneath the counter!

Thankfully, the staffer did not see me! But I feel he should have made a more thorough check for the child under the counter… there could have been a child there and he should have been more concerned….oh balderdash! Biffy stopped her train of thought and murmured, "Anyways, I have work to do!"

She quickly jumped up to the front desk and grabbed the laptop!

Guess what? The laptop was on. *And Shweta's account still open!*

Great! Biffy inwardly rejoiced.

In fact, a conversation seemed to be on in a chat room.

The last words were "What is that clanging?'

Biffy peered to read who had written message. It said: "Savvyior. m@…!

"Gotcha..same one!" Biffy muttered, hitting the keys!

"What clanging?" Biffy rapidly typed in. No one saw her hidden or when she grabbed the laptop to nestle it in her lap as she crouched under the counter when the lobby was in an uproar.

"I thought I heard something!" came a message.

"Sir…Sir, I need to meet you….please something very important has come up. I have to tell you personally.." Biffy furiously typed, hoping her message sounded like that giddy headed Shweta!

"You know the rules", came a type back.

"Yes but…this is important.."

"OK, come all the way up…use the stairway not the lift."

Leaving the laptop back in its place, Biffy ran back to Kalra's office. The hotel was still completely deserted. The loud siren of a fire engine sounded outside. Biffy barely made it as the firemen rushed in.

Her sisters were relieved to see her.

"I got contact. The "Master" is in the hotel…he said come all the way up..use the stairway.….now which room…?" Biffy chewed her underlip and thought hard.

"Let's investigate!" Miffy suggested.

"Huh huh!" They moved the cupboard and again went through the hidden doorway. More comfortably, this time though!

Biffy remembered to replace the cupboard and lock the door, hanging the keys back. The girls scrambled up the back stairs. They went to all the floors connected by these service stairs. They were preceding the firemen who too were checking for fire. The firemen halted at the first floor as they reached the broken fire alarm window. Coming to the conclusion that some horrible vandalism had broken the glass and set off the alarm, they gave a thorough check on all three floors. "No panic…if there is a fire, the smoke alarm sensors go off after some minutes of the alarm and the water sprinklers go on.. here only the alarm has gone off…I hope the hotel was not practising a drill? It is common to set off this alarm for fire drill purposes, is it not?" the chief fireman asked Mr Sud.

Questions, explanations filled the air. But with no conclusion to explain the confusion! The hotel was filling up with guest once more!

Meanwhile,the Trips slowly climbed each floor. Finally,they reached the roof and faced a metal door. It was ajar.

Biffy signalled that she wanted to check the roof too. Very

stealthily, she nudged it open. The door led them onto a huge terrace with the water tank towers and littered with half broken sticks, brooms and debris. Tentatively, the Trips moved forward.

On her return, Shweta glanced at her laptop and wondered why Sir had switched off. That stupid maid...she kept troubling everyone, "My girls, my girls"! Shweta mimicked in her mind. Hah ah, where will she find her girls? Let us see..ha ha! Shweta smirked inwardly.

Suddenly sobering and shrugging, she began working on her desk computer

Whilst Malti had lured Shweta away, Mr Lal had returned downstairs and joined Mrs Lal outside. Mrs Lal, caught up in the moments that every noisy alarm begets, barely acknowledged her husband's sudden return. Instead, she told him that she was worried about her girls. Somehow, he managed to give her the slip and sought Malti out again. His mind was abuzz with what Malti was relating now; she explained why she had stalled telling him that the girls were in Mr Kalra's office when she met Mr Lal on the first floor. "Biffy said..." And Malti conveyed Biffy's concerns of raising no suspicions! Mr Lal quietly followed Malti back into the hotel and into the offices. Surveying the hidden door, the same one the girls had just exited from, "Well I'll be...!" Mr Lal muttered.

"It opens from the inside...we need to go up from here... if it is all right, sir....!" Malti deferentially suggested, moving aside to let him pass.

"Click-clickk-click!" The faint sounds of someone typing came from the vicinity of the roof where the Trips were stealthily sneaking forward.

"The sound is coming from there," Biffy whispered.

"Miffy, you go behind that beam... stay there." Miffy nodded and darted to hide behind the beam. "Piffy, you go to the other side and hide too, I am going in!"

Piffy too darted and hid.

Keeping close to the water tank walls, Biffy inched towards the sounds of typing.

As she turned the curve of the wall, she was faced with a room that had a metal door!

The typing was clearer. Who can even think of coming up here….the roof… clever thief! Biffy thought, as she confronted the door and considered her next move.

"Creakkkkkkkkkkkk" the metal door opened.

Biffy dived behind a jutting mass of wall. Slowly, she peeped out, "Gasp!"

The kabadiwala called Anwar, hoisting a sack, came out! He shut the door, and whistling, made his way forward. Instead of using the way that Biffy had come by, he went straight towards the opposite wall, leapt over and disappeared. Holding her breath, Biffy waited, then slowly sneaked to the edge of the wall and peeped over. *A spiral staircase* hugged the back wall of the hotel!?!!

One connecting stairway on each back landing, right till the bottom! Biffy quickly drew back because Anwar was still descending!

The mystery deepens!

Biffy went straight to the door and opened it. It was an alcove of some sorts. There was an odd shaped opening in front. Biffy bent and moved inside the alcove. It was big enough so she could easily walk through! She saw an arch and came into a *huge fully furnished room!*

"Click click click!" right in front on a desk, face hidden by the laptop cover, someone sat typing.

Biffy dived behind an armchair.

Her breath stopped when she stretched to peek over the laptop cover and saw who was there.

Mr Kalra! Mr Kalra, hale and hearty, sat looking intently at the laptop screen.

Biffy bit her lips so as to not gasp out aloud!

She darted behind the chaise lounge and kept very still.

Someone had entered. Anwar the kabadiwala had returned.

But? From where? I came from here, Anwar has quickly returned …um there must be another entry point to this room! Biffy's mind buzzed.

"Anwar, Shewta was coming up… has not arrived yet… said something important…..what could it be?" Mr Kalra said

Anwar muttered something.

"But according to our plans she does not come up at all…I am to be moved tomorrow- ….er do they all still believe the kidnapping yarn (chuckle)…..anyways…yes, here is what you need to do…" again click -click –click! The typing began.

Rolling silently, Biffy reached the alcove. With a swift movement, she ran out. Once out, she called out loudly to her sisters.

"Miffy-Piffy, hurry we….!"

"Oh, so you are here…!" Mr Lal's voice boomed right next to her!

"Papa, thank God…?!?"

Mr Lal and Malti had come up to the roof.

Piffy, Miffy too had joined them. Papa Lal had been grilling the sisters when Biffy had come up!

Breathlessly, Biffy informed them of what she saw. *"Papa, Mr Kalra staged his own kidnapping!"*

"Why, the snivelling….!" Outraged Mr Lal, in a completely rash and thoughtless overreaction rushed forward and flung open the metal door; he hurried in through the alcove entrance, chased by Malti, Biffy, Miffy and *Piffy!*

To say Mr Kalra was surprised would be an understatement. Mr Lal charged at him. The girls and Malti charged at Anwar who tried to run from the alcove. Biffy grabbed his legs to throw him down, Piffy managed his flaying hands and Miffy sat on him. Anwar was befuddled already, seeing three exactly alike little people, so it was easy for the Trips!

As for Malti? She generally squeaked and squawked in a nervous dither around them!

Mr Kalra was pressed backward and fell down onto the desk, with Mr Lal on top. In complete surprise, and an absolutely unscheduled follow up, this is what happened next:

"AAAAARGH-STOP!"

Mr Lal felt cold metal pushing back his nostrils! He jumped away rubbing his tickling nose!

Mr Kalra had whipped out a loaded gun from the desk!

He again snarled warningly; now standing and waving a gun at his uninvited guests: "Stop or I kill each one of you!"

Horror writ all over his face, Mr Lal backed off, saying slowly, "Hey man, relax, mind the kids, that is dangerous!"

"Yeah-sneaking, interfering @#$%*&^%$#)(*&! Kids...no devils....!#@%^$&*!" Kalra spewed swear words and the girls blushed.

Anwar stood dusting himself. He looked very sheepish/confused and dazed.

No one, yes no one, could think of the drama followed next!

From somewhere, a bullet shot forward in the shape of ROCK!

And Mrs Lal!

Yes! Mama Lal came up from thin air, shouting "Leave my family alone!" "whup" a stick, half broken, felled Kalra; the gun went scattering, "tup tup tup *and tup!*" over the uneven flooring. Taking a deep breath, Mrs Lal triumphantly smiled, then with a kind of edgy nervousness, peered down to see what she had done!

Sigh! Actually her "whup" had knocked Mr Kalra out cold!!!?!!!

Not used to perpetuating such violence, Mrs Lal burst into tears. Mr Lal rushed to her! "I saw you going into Mr Kalra's office from the windows," she sobbed to her husband. "I came inside too! Then I saw the hidden door and....."

"Hush-hush!" Mr Lal calmed her.

Meanwhile, the girls and Malti, on cue, grabbed Anwar! Rock with his tiny mouth nibbled Mr Kalra's ankles as he lay moaning on the ground!

"Thanks, Mommy!" Biffy's shout trilled in the air!

"Call security…..!"

"Let go-ooo of me….!"

"I hit so hard-did not mean to? boo hoooo…..!"

"We are proud of you dear…"

"Tie them up…."

"How……"

"What a situation….!"

"Wooofffffff….."

"Hello, this is Mr Lal…immediately send up security to…."

"Aieeeeee"

These were the words floating up from each…conscious…individual present! The last squeak being from an overexcited Malti! Yes, and as for the unconscious individual, Mr Kalra, he just went *"ummmmm"* lolling his head on the floor.

The security was quickly summoned and the crooks hauled up! Shweta was nabbed laptop and all, and Mrs Kalra with her swish packed luggage! That they were shocked at the twist in events is an understatement!

Sixteen

"Amazing to hear the Trips nabbed a crook—*once again!?*", Dadaji proudly smiled at his son. The Trips and their parents had left Delhi and were in Mumbai on the last leg of their holidays, as planned. The Trips were thrilled to be staying with their grandparents!

Mr Lal's father or Dadaji, surveyed them as they sat before him early in the morning. Over their first tea cup (for the grown-ups) and chocolate milk (for the girls), the entire incident was related amidst good humour!

"It was a deep dark cyber crime spilling over to more sinister smuggling!" Mr Lal informed Dadaji, while Dadima paid full attention. By now, the Trips fussed around Rock, running in and out; Mrs Lal and Malti decided to leave for a walk. Papa, of course, was regaling his parents with an account of the whole affair.

"Mr Kalra, the manager, along with his wife Mrs Kalra, Shweta, his receptionist and Anwar, who incidentally is a junk dealer, hatched an evil plan. Mrs Kalra, it turns out, has very expensive tastes!" Mr Lal said in an explanatory tone!

"Mr Kalra initially began stealing credit card details from our guests. He improved on his crime by even hacking into guest e-mails. He would offer up some amazing deals/lotteries and certain details so the innocent guest would give the details of his or her credit card. Once they had that, Shweta and Kalra moved in. Anwar was a soft 'dealer'. He, of course, was not involved in the card crime. He pedalled all the petty thefts being allowed by Kalra without suspicion to junk dealers at good rates! So Kalra and his cohorts' were multi-tasking in their offence files! Meaning, they were stealing hotel goods, stealing money from the tiller and, side by side, continuing with their cyber crimes!"

"Why did he begin the kidnap drama...I mean he was getting away with his own... but why the girls?" Dadaji wanted to know.

"Kalra had himself kidnapped to extract a large sum from the hotel via his wife who was in on the crimes too. The threat about bringing a stain on the hotel reputation worked. Petty crimes, disgruntled guests are a nightmare for any hotel management, believe me! Both husband/ wife thieving team planned to run away to South America and resettle there. In the greed for more money and so that his felony was not exposed, he kidnapped the girls!"

"But an educated man and his wife with such low grade intentions...." Dadima's voice trailed.

"They shamelessly swiped cards!"

"How? The guests have the cards right?"

"Kalra would befriend a particular guest. When the guest would be leaving, a night before, Kalra would ask for the credit card, stating some reason, about billing, etc. Till recently, before the greedy group became so careless, once in four months a credit card was filched from a carefully checked out guest. Now every time, it was not done the same way. Sometimes, he would directly take the card for the hotel charges, etc. Sometimes, he would get Anwar to actually pick the pocket of the guest and steal the wallet from the targeted guest outside the hotel... the racket was so well entrenched, the kingpin being Kalra and his wife! Kalra then played hero. He would 'find' the wallet minus the foreign currency but with all the cards intact and return it to the guest. His request not to go to the police gained further respect once he did that, you know, find the wallet! The guest would be impressed! Since the wallet was stolen outside the hotel, no one suspected the hotel or that the card had been used. The guests trusted him."

"So what did they do with the card?" Dadi asked.

"*Ma*, once they had the card, they went shopping. Mostly, they chose a time when the guest had a flight in the early hours; the victim never suspected, since he was given the card and the hotel bills promptly before he left! In his rush to reach the airport, he only came to know of his loss when he was back home, abroad. Now these chosen tourists from whom they were to steal were also checked out. Most came from remote European countries. Not wanting trouble, they usually did not report the theft! And if anyone did report it, the complaint came to Mr Kalra and he squashed it! There and then, so nothing actually came out!"

"How smart!"

"In fact, earlier when we had just arrived, Biffy followed Mr Kalra out of the hotel. He was on a shopping trip with a guest's card!"

"My God!" Dadaji exclaimed.

"That is not all. Shweta would sneak into the rooms when the guests were asleep and steal the cards. She would slip them back after swiping them whereever she wanted before they woke up!"

"Really?"

"Hu huh, the hotel provided a good cover plan. When renovations took place, a certain portion was walled in. Now rooms 101, 102, 103 had the door leading into the walled in areas, going right up to the roof! Kalra discovered this. He never, never assigned these rooms to guests!"

"Oh, so the goods of the hotel were sneaked out to the roof or the room the Trips were in and Anwar used the spiral stairs to dispose of them!" Dadaji, who had heard some of the story earlier, provided.

Mr Lal nodded, "Exactly! This went on for two years. Kalra, being the manager, kept a lid on things and, surprisingly, no one reported anything! Only Biffy smelled out the hanky-panky and he was exposed!"

"Don't forget, Shweta never left her laptop alone!" Biffy bounced into the room to say.

"Yes, because she was constantly sending fake e-mails of lottery wins to the mails she had hacked into."

"So how did they make money?" Dadima asked.

"Simple Dadima, they would fool the guest in his own e-mail to say that to send the lottery ticket, they needed a certain amount of money in the account numbers they were giving. Whenever the guest bit the bait, the crooks were richer by some dollars/ euros!"

Dadima looked shocked.

"Shweta even had this ongoing communication with a young boy in Algiers. She hacked his mail ID and sent him a mail saying he had inherited money. Since she was the bequeather's legal aide, she had to be paid her fees and also she would help in smoothening the transactions with her expert advice!"

"She hacked into Biffy's mail too!" Papa Lal added!

"She sure is sorry she did that!" Biffy exclaimed coming into the room.

The conversation became noisier as the girls returned; so did Mrs Lal and the family went into a loud chattering mode.....